THIS PARODY OF DEATH

An Ashmole Foxe Georgian Mystery

WILLIAM SAVAGE

Ridge&Bourne

For my Family, especially Jenn

I

THE DANDY

It had been a long, hard winter, the roads treacherous with ice and snow. Food prices kept rising, driving many of the poor to the edge of starvation. Even now, as April tottered towards May, the sun rarely appeared from behind the clouds. Rain soaked the fields, still sodden from snow, and bitter winds drove in from the German Ocean. What had kept the inhabitants of Norwich from total misery had been the fortitude of the crews on the coal-ships from Newcastle. They usually stopped sailing between November and March. The seas were too dangerous. This year, most had kept at sea, making sure of the extra supplies of coal needed. Many had paid for such bravery with their lives. In the worst storms, scores of vessels went down on the reefs and shoals off the Norfolk coast.

Mr Ashmole Foxe stood in front of the mirror in his dressing room. He had told Molly to light the fire in the small grate. The east wind, a fixture so far this year, was sending acrid smoke into the room. He had spent a fortune on coals, yet the house was still full of draughts and cold corners. Even his bed had felt cold last night, despite the warming pan laid in it.

Foxe examined himself with the attention of a connoisseur. His gaze travelled from his neck to his feet and he shifted his body left and right to take in every angle. Then he turned and peered at himself over his shoulder to see how he appeared from the side. All the while, his frown deepened into a scowl.

This was his best and newest suit. A coat of finest brown velvet, the front thick with embroidered flowers and scrolls in gold and silver wire. Buttons plated with gold and embossed with *Fleur de Lis*. Long cuffs decorated in matching mode and bearing the same golden buttons. Breeches made of finest kid leather, with a broad line of embroidery down the front of each leg. Under his coat, a cream-coloured waistcoat, patterned all over with sprays of tiny leaves and flowers in bright colours. A snowy shirt and stock at the throat and pink silk stockings of the highest quality. Then, a final touch, provided by maroon leather shoes with broad golden buckles enriched with silver filigree.

It was a magnificent ensemble in the very height of fashion. A suit which would have drawn the eye in any theatre, assembly room or dining salon in the capital.

That was the trouble. It was too fine and fashionable for dull, old Norwich. Norfolk people took years to catch up with the clothes worn by the *ton* in London, even the women. By the time they did, what they thought of as fashionable was long out of date at Vauxhall Gardens or in the grand houses of The Strand.

Fox turned back to face the mirror and sighed. He had suffered two serious blows to his pride the day before. It began when his partner in the business of selling books, Mrs Crombie, had taken delivery of a fresh set of prints and caricatures. These were a perennial source of profit, so she hurried to fix some up in the windows of the shop. There they could be admired by passers-by and potential purchasers. Several of these caricatures had featured the fashionable young men known as 'macaronis'. The name came from the showy Italianate manners they affected. The artist had portrayed them as willowy, effete fops or dandies. Two pulled on the lacing of a corset that was deforming the waist of a third into that of a wasp. In another print, three fanned a friend who had fainted at the sight of a plum pudding and a foaming tankard of ale. All wore stocks so high and tight that their faces peered over the top like mice emerging from a hole. Foreign styles and manners mocked in the traditional English way.

It chanced as Foxe passed by, that a group of eager people clustered outside the shop were enjoying the free entertainment. He heard one call out that he knew Mr Foxe was vain, but he never thought he'd take to covering the windows of his shop with pictures of himself. The others roared with laughter at this. Another called out, "Aye. That's right enough. He's vainer than a strutting rooster. Likes his hens too." More guffaws. Now another joined in. "He's more foppish than these fellows though," he yelled. "I reckons his tailor must be damn near blind to dress him up like that." More yells and catcalls followed. Some began arguing which character in the caricatures most resembled the owner of the shop.

Foxe buried his face in the collar of his thick topcoat and hurried on, his face flaming. He cared nothing for the ignorant criticism of these country louts, he told himself, but, by God, he wasn't going to suffer open ridicule in his own city.

Worse was to follow. That same evening, Foxe went to the theatre, as he did at least once every week when the company was offering productions. His taste for young and pretty actresses was well known and he tried to cast his eyes over whoever was the latest to grace the city's fine theatre. Now his last choice, Lily, had moved away to Bath, he was on the hunt again.

To his delight, the latest addition to the Norwich Company of Comedians proved to be a stunning beauty. Slightly older than Lily, he judged, but with a fine soprano voice and a figure that had the young blades in the stalls in a ferment of whistles and blown kisses. After the performance ended, the manager took Mr Foxe backstage himself. Foxe was a generous patron to the theatre. There was no possibility of leaving him to fight his way through the mass of admirers besieging the actresses' dressing room.

Close up, Miss Isobel Smith — for so the manager introduced her — was even lovelier than Foxe had thought.

"This, my dear Miss Smith," the manager said, "is Mr Ashmole Foxe, a great friend to this theatre and company and a true ornament to this fine city."

All quite excessive, no doubt, but theatrical people were prone to hyperbole.

Miss Smith looked him up and down, took in the gorgeous decoration and fine fabric of his ensemble and burst out laughing. For a moment, Foxe was stunned, then he turned and walked out, followed by the manager in such a state of agitation that he could scarcely speak.

It wasn't surprising that the shame of the encounter, together with the coldness of his room, meant Foxe had tossed and turned all night. The dandified image was what he was known for. He had built it up to encourage those he wished to catch to underrate the man within. No more, it seemed. It had failed him. It was one thing to be underestimated, quite another to be mocked and jeered at. It needed to go, as did this, his newest suit of clothes. Well, maybe not go. It would be fine in the right context. Just not in the streets of Norwich.

With a shrug, he reached his decision. The image of the thoughtless rake would no longer do. Times were changing and he was getting too old to act that part without provoking mirth. He might still draw envious eyes at the Mayor's ball in a fine outfit, especially with a beautiful woman on his arm. At ten o'clock on a Saturday morning in Norwich, he needed to blend in, not stand out like a parrot amongst sparrows.

After a final grunt and several muttered curses, he called Alfred, his manservant, to bring him his most sombre clothes and help him change. He would be late in setting out for his daily visit to his favourite coffeehouse, but it couldn't be helped.

Every morning, save Sundays, Mr Foxe took coffee and read the London papers that had arrived fresh on the stagecoach. Next, he took a stroll through the streets around Norwich's vast Market Place. Today he was still at the head of his own stairs, clad in a suit of sober dark fustian, when he heard a loud knocking at the front door.

Molly, his head housemaid, hastened to answer this frantic summons. That it had not put her in the best of moods was obvious from her first words to the lad she found was the source of all the commotion.

"Trying to break the door down, are you? Well? What's so important you have to raise half the neighbourhood with your foolishness?"

"I got to speak to Mr Foxe —" the boy began.

"Oh, have you? Have you indeed? And why's that? The Guildhall burned down? Cathedral in ruins? He ain't in to the likes of you, so you can go back to whatever hovel you crawled out of."

"I got to speak to him, so you tell him that. You're only a maid, not the mistress of the house. You do as I — yow!"

Molly, driven to fury by his impudence, fetched him a hearty slap across the side of his head. Since she had grown of late into a sturdy young woman, the boy staggered and all but fell over. It was time to intervene.

"Thank you, Molly," Foxe said, in as calm a voice as he could muster through his smothered laughter. "Let's find out what he has to say before you knock him senseless. Well, boy? You wanted Mr Foxe. Here I am."

Molly drew aside, but did not step back far, her anger still unsatisfied. The boy, aware of this, stayed well back.

"Don't worry," Foxe said. "You're safe so long as I'm here. Now, what is it you want?"

"My master sent me, your worship. He says you're to come as fast as you can."

"Does he, by George? It seems he's as eager to give orders as you are. Who is he then and what's so urgent. Speak up, or I'll turn Molly loose on you again."

The boy gulped and edged as far away from Molly as he could. "Mr George Tate, the grocer," he said. "He's my master ... and it's about a murder."

"Murder?" Foxe said, showing no surprise. "Not of Mr Tate, I trust. I've bought from him for many a year, as my father did before me. It would be most vexing to have to find a new grocer to deal with."

"Nah, your worship. My master's alive and well, only right put out over this affair. It's old misery-face Logan who's bin done in. Killed with a great knife, they say, and lying in a pool of blood."

"Stop that at once," Molly said. "He's Mr Logan to you. Lord, Sir, listen to the mouth on him. Needs a good whipping, if you ask me."

"Maybe," Foxe agreed, "but not here or from you. Perhaps you should return to your duties and let me deal with this, Molly. Off you go now. Right boy. Where was Mr Logan stabbed?"

"In the ringing chamber, your worship."

"In the — that wasn't quite what I meant, but it's a start. Where on his body?"

"In the throat, my master says. Right across his windpipe."

"And he was in the ringing chamber of the tower at the time. Of which church?"

"St. Peter Mancroft. He be — I mean he were — the Tower Captain. My master's one of the United Norwich Ringers. I reckon he'll be the captain now."

"The bell ringing team. Tell me, boy, do you know why your master sent you to find me?"

"He come back to our shop in a rare taking, your worship. The United Norwich Ringers was supposed to ring a long peal tomorrow to celebrate something or other — I forgets what. They bin practising for months. Now it's all off. The constable came to our shop right early and told him that. Said Old Logan — Mr Logan — 'ad been murdered and the coroner would have to come, then bring his jury to see the body. Tower's closed for two days at least. My master was powerful upset. That's when Captain Brock, who happened to be in the shop at the time, said he ought to talk to you. You'd know what to do, he said."

"So, I have Captain Brock to thank for this, have I? I'll speak to him later."

"My master says he would have come to you himself, only he's got to stay in his shop, it being the day of the market and all. He said I was to 'pologise for the incon ... incon ... for troubling you, your worship."

"Tell your master that I will come later this morning, after I've had my coffee and taken my morning walk. If Mr Logan is dead and the authorities involved, there's no need to upset my morning further. Here's a penny for your trouble and some words of advice."

"Yes, your worship?"

"Never annoy a woman early in the morning. They're never at their best before noon and it gives them all day to make you suffer for it. Now, be off with you. I'll be round to see your master in an hour or so."

2

MURDER

Outside, it could have been January. The few people who were about walked heads down and hunched against the wind, wrapped in their thickest clothes. Fortunately, Foxe didn't have far to go, or he might well have turned back to the warmth of his own fireside. Damn the weather! He was in a gloomy mood anyway. Now this foul wind threatened to sink him even further into melancholy.

He'd never expected to become rich. Never sought it. It had crept up on him somehow. Once you had wealth, it seemed you couldn't help making more, unless you threw your money away on drink or gambling, of course, like the Earl of Pentelow. Foxe had no taste for either. Women might help you spend it, but the kind who feigned affection in return for gold and jewels repelled him. He decided he was, at root, exactly what his birth suggested; a member of that wide group of people generally called the 'middling sort', industrious, thrifty and bent on leaving some sort of achievement behind to mark their presence in the world. Unfortunately, he had no idea what that might be.

You couldn't escape your nature, of course. He should have known that. Look at his old friend Brock. When he first retired from active service in the Royal Navy, he tried to set himself up as a blunt, no-nonsense wherry captain. Then, he had cultivated common speech and concealed his past as much as he could. It didn't work. Now, thanks to his friendship with Lady Henfield, his fine manners were returning and he spoke as a gentleman and retired naval post-captain should.

Foxe sighed so deeply that a passing servant girl decided that the gentleman had doubtless been crossed in love and was probably on his way to drown himself in the Wensum.

For a time, buying and selling rare books had amused him, but the lustre had worn off, leaving only another way of adding to his wealth. Mrs Crombie ran his shop with almost no help from him — did it better than he had ever done, or his father before him. His properties brought in a steady income from rents and his joint shipping business with Brock was flourishing. He had nothing to do and all the time in the world to do it. He was barely thirty years of age. Decades of prosperous boredom stretched ahead.

When at last Foxe arrived at the coffeehouse, Captain Brock was already there, sitting at what Foxe regarded as 'his' table and reading 'his' London paper.

"Morning, Foxe," Brock said. "Bitter wind again. If the weather doesn't change soon, the price of corn will be even higher than it was last year. Farmers can't get on their land in weather like this. The seed goes in late and the seedlings don't grow away as they should. Wouldn't be surprised to see the poor folk rioting and trying to take it out on the millers and corn chandlers."

Foxe ignored this and began to complain about Brock foisting the investigation of the murder of Logan on him. Brock cut him off.

"Why? Not doing anything else, are you? Halloran hasn't asked you to get involved in anything? Nobody banging on your door wanting you to look into anything else? This seems right up your street. Besides, it's almost on your doorstep."

Foxe had to admit all that was true, but it didn't mean he was keen to rush into another mystery. Brock was unimpressed.

"You're getting lazy, Foxe. Mrs Crombie's got that bookshop of yours running so nicely on her own you've nothing to do all day. Do you good to have something to occupy your mind."

"My mind doesn't need your help, Brock. Stick to your own business and keep your nose out of mine."

"Got out of bed the wrong side this morning, eh? Missing Lily? Here's a nice little murder waiting for the great Mr Foxe to solve it and you sit there finding excuses. Has to be some reason why you turn up looking like a rich parson, instead of a fashionable young rake."

This was too close to the bone for Foxe, who burst out in a rare display of temper. "Oh, so I'm an overdressed young fop, am I? A macaroni? I'll have you know, Captain Brock—"

"Hold on, Foxe. I never said that. All I asked was why you're in sober clothes this morning, compared with your normal style."

"People outside my shop," Foxe said. "Mrs Crombie's put some new caricatures in the window that make fun of London fops and macaronis. You know the style. As I was walking past, I heard someone say I was so vain I was now posting pictures of myself in my shop windows. Everyone laughed."

"Why not?" Brock said. "Sounds funny to me."

"But why? Why make such comments about me? I know I try to be fashionable."

"Fashionable for London, not for Norwich. Look, Foxe. A few folk are amused by your clothes and make jokes about you. It's not the end of the world. You ought to fit your ideas of fashion to where you live, instead of the capital."

"That wasn't all."

But Brock wasn't at all sympathetic when he heard the tale of Miss Smith. For several minutes, he was laughing so much he could barely get his breath.

"That's made my day," he said at last. "The great lover bested by some chit of a girl. Wonderful." He pulled a large kerchief out of his coat pocket and wiped his eyes. "You had it coming to you, Foxe. Actresses these days take their art more seriously than they used to. You can't assume their only reason for going on stage is to lure rich men into bed with them. They have more important things to think about, like their acting careers."

"Could have both."

"Probably don't much want to put up with rich men pawing them about. Some of the old goats who hang around that theatre would put any woman off."

"Are you suggesting I'm an old—"

"I wasn't suggesting anything. If you can't take a joke, we'd better change the subject. When are you planning to talk with Tate the grocer?"

"About noon." Foxe answered without thinking.

"You fraud! All these complaints when you're already on the scent. Good man, George Tate. Needs your help. Logan has no family to seek out his killer. Tate and the other United Norwich Ringers are the closest things to relatives he had, only they don't know what to do to smoke out who murdered him. I said you'd tell them."

"And what are you going to do to help?"

"Not a lot, this time. I've got other matters to attend to. Well, must be off. Busy day ahead. Tell you all about it another time."

⚜

Foxe reached Mr Tate's grocery shop as the bells in Norwich's many churches were disagreeing about the exact moment of noon. Despite being late in the day for shopping, the shop was doing a brisk trade. Knots of servants stood outside exchanging gossip. Others leaned over the sacks of meal and trestle tables loaded with eggs and dried fruit, peering through the leaded panes of the windows. For most servants, taking a list of requirements to one of the city's shops was their only opportunity to speak with someone outside their own household. They didn't want to miss anyone they knew. Besides, the murder was the best topic for gossip in many a day.

Here and there a busy cook or housewife pushed her way through the throng, all sharp elbows and disapproval. When Foxe entered, those who recognised him were already whispering to their neighbours. By the end of the day, everyone in the city would know where he'd been.

Mr Tate must have been keeping a watch for his visitor. He pushed forwards at once, leaving an elderly cook with her list in her hand and her mouth still open. Like his shop, the proprietor had an old-fashioned exterior. He wore a long white apron over his dusty waistcoat with an elderly wig askew on his head. Within, however, he was all business and bustle. Now he hurried Foxe into the back of the shop, past piles of goods laid out for display and sacks of coffee beans still fragrant from roasting. There they went through a door at the further side from the street into a neat and well-furnished parlour.

Tate offered Foxe coffee or chocolate. "Our best quality, Mr Foxe. Finest you'll ever taste. We don't sell it to everyone."

Foxe was already full of coffee, so he chose chocolate. It was everything Mr Tate said it was. The grocer took some himself, watching to see his guest's reaction.

"This is very fine chocolate," Foxe said. "I'll have to tell my cook to get some next time we run out."

Mr Tate was delighted. He clapped his pudgy hands together and beamed. Then he recovered himself and assumed a grave expression.

"My condolences, Mr Foxe," he said.

Foxe stared at him. "Condolences? For what?"

"I thought you must have suffered a family bereavement. Your clothes ..."

Did everyone judge him by what he happened to be wearing at the time? It was too annoying.

"Mr Logan has been murdered, your boy said. In the church —"

"Not in the church, sir. In the ringing chamber of the tower." Mr Tate was a stickler for accuracy.

"In the ringing chamber then. Who found his body?"

Once he was fixed on a topic, George Tate was one of those people who couldn't bear to leave a single detail out. "The ringing chamber is the lowest room in the tower, Mr Foxe. It's got a high ceiling to allow the next chamber, the one holding the bells, to be placed just below the tower roof on a level with the slatted windows that let the sound out. The higher up they are, the further the sound spreads. Our bells —"

If he wasn't interrupted, he'd explain every rope, frame and ladder.

"Who found the man's body?" Foxe repeated.

Mr Tate looked hurt. "I'm telling you, aren't I? It was the watchman. He came by the church as it was getting light and noticed the west door was open a little way. That's the one in the tower that lets you into the place where the stairway —"

Now he was going to describe the church layout. It would be the stonework next and then the stained glass.

"So he went in," Foxe said.

Another frown. Mr Tate did not like to be hurried. "Aye, he did. Thought some vagabonds might have taken the chance to bed down in the church. Always some hanging about the Market Place. They like to sleep anywhere they can get out of the wind. Some of them build little shelters in corners —"

Heaven help us all! If Foxe didn't stop him he was going to explain the sleeping habits of Norwich's tramps and drunkards. It was enough to drive a man insane.

"Were there any?"

"What?"

"Vagabonds in the church?"

"No. Well … there may have been, I suppose, but the watchman never got that far. As soon as he was inside, he saw the door that leads to the stairs up the tower was open. That's always kept shut and locked. Safety, see? Bells are dangerous things if you play about with them. A few years ago —"

"He went up?"

"Of course he did. Might be someone messing about up there. Took him a while too. He's an old man and not strong in his wind."

Most of the city's watchmen were old. The pay was poor and younger people didn't want to be wandering the streets at night in all weathers. This particular watchman must be unusually bold. They generally ran away from anything that might be dangerous.

"When he got to the ringing chamber he found Richard Logan lying there in a great pool of blood. Blood everywhere. It'll take hours to clean it up."

"What did the watchman do next?"

"Went back down the stairs a good deal quicker than he came up. Then ran out into the street, shaking his clapper and yelling 'Murder! Murder!' at the top of his lungs. That fetched a good crowd even that early."

"And then?" It was infuriating. You either got everything, or had to drag things out of him. When he was describing things of no importance, Mr Tate rattled on and on. Once he got to what mattered, he kept stopping and staring at Foxe as if he had no idea what to say next.

"All the commotion brought one of the constables. He took charge. Sent someone to tell the magistrate what had happened. Then he had the good sense to send for me as well."

"Not the Vicar?"

"Tower isn't much business of the parson's, is it?"

"Not in his own church?" Foxe was amazed.

"Not really. I suppose he has some say about the stonework, but that's all. Chancel is the parson's business. Rest of the church is up to the churchwardens to look after. The tower and the bells are our concern. Can't trust a parson, see? Some of them would have the bells melted down and sold, if they could. Not many parsons who understand proper ringing — or like it either. All they want is a noise to tell people to come to church."

"So, they sent for you."

"I'm one of the churchwardens. Besides, a fair few around here know I'm also a leading light in the United Norwich Ringers."

"That's the bell-ringers of the church?"

"Aye, It's our home tower. Got one of the finest ring of bells in the country, St. Peter Mancroft. And the finest group of ringers, though I say it myself. Our band started in —"

"So, you went to see what was going on?"

"I knew that already, didn't I? They told me poor old Logan was dead in a pool of blood. Said it when they came here. Right mess it is too. Won't be able to ring our peal the day after tomorrow. We've been practicing for months. Logan was our Tower Captain and called the changes. Don't know what we'll do without him."

Foxe let these strange terms pass him by for the present. It wouldn't do to set Mr Tate off on lengthy explanations. He'd find out what he needed to know from someone else.

"Do you know how Mr Logan died?"

"Had his throat cut from ear to ear." Mr Tate spoke as if Logan should have had the good manners to die in a neater way. The mess bothered him more than the man's death, by the sound of it.

All this time had been taken to get to the simple fact that the man's throat was cut. Nothing about why he was in the ringing chamber. No suggestion of what Foxe was expected to do. At this rate, they'd be there until dinner time.

Fortunately for Foxe's sanity, Mrs Tate chose that moment to come into the parlour and take charge. Perhaps she knew that fifteen minutes of her husband's explanations was all most people could take. She sent her husband back into his shop, where she said Lord Suffield's housekeeper was waiting for him, and got right to the point.

"Thank you for coming, Mr Foxe. This business has upset my husband a good deal. He was sick when he came back from the church. Well, you would be, wouldn't you? Not often you see a man with his throat cut."

Foxe supposed that was so.

"Someone needs to find out who did such a terrible thing and Mr Logan has no family anyone knows of. The bell ringers are all the family he seemed to want. He didn't marry. Too wrapped up in the silly business of change-ringing, like my husband. Aside from his shop, most of Mr Tate's thoughts revolve around St. Peter Mancroft's bells. His children and I come a very poor third."

She seemed quite cheerful about it.

"What I'm not sure, Mrs Tate, is what your husband wants me to do."

"Bless him, he doesn't know that himself. When it comes to grocery, he's a demon for order and detail. Same with his bells. For the rest, he hasn't much idea. He realises something needs to be done, of course. That's why, when Captain Brock mentioned you, he was so relieved. He wants you to tell him what to do, not the other way around. He's terrified the others will expect him to track down the murderer."

"But I'm still not at all clear on what happened," Foxe said. "I know nothing about bells, Tower Captains or any of the other words your husband threw at me."

"Keep it that way if you'll take my advice." Mrs Tate smiled. "Give any of that bunch a chance to talk about bells or change-ringing and you'll hear far more than any mortal could wish. Let me see if I can help you." She sat herself in one of the chairs and beamed at her visitor.

"Richard Logan has been found murdered in the ringing chamber of the church. He is — was — the Tower Captain, and they had a ringing practice yesterday evening. I expect he had stayed behind to make sure all was left in good order."

"So, he was a kind of chief bell-ringer?"

"That's it exactly. The ringers form a team. Can't ring changes on your own. They choose a team name — these call themselves The United Norwich Ringers. Then they elect a Captain, who's usually the most experienced ringer. Mr Logan was nigh on sixty years of age and had been ringing since he was a schoolboy. The Tower Captain organises and leads the band, choosing which peals they should ring and who should handle which bell."

"Now I understand. That's why your husband implied his death was a bad blow to the whole group."

"Indeed. They'll be lost for a while. The team's almost a family for many of them, and Mr Logan was its father. I'm sure they'll handle everything necessary for the funeral, though Logan's own workers will do the details."

"Why's that?"

Mrs Tate stared. "Didn't you know? Mr Logan was a carpenter, undertaker and coffin maker. In his father's day, the business used to be the best in Norwich, or so they say."

"Used to be?"

"That business has been declining for years, ever since his father died. James Logan was a brilliant man who died far too young. His son was never a match, either as a carpenter or a businessman. In the end, all he had left was the undertaking side."

"If Mr Logan's workers can handle the funeral and the authorities are well aware of what has happened, I suppose my role in the affair is to find the killer."

"Exactly right. Bring the wretch before the magistrate and see justice is done. Captain Brock said you're a rare one to ferret out a criminal. Oh, I'm sure the magistrates will offer the usual reward, but it's not their job to seek out the murderer, is it? Usually the victim's family take that on, or find someone to do it for them. The magistrate has no part until the person accused is brought before him."

"Your husband wants me to find who killed Richard Logan? A man I never knew?"

"That's right. None of the ringers have the first notion of how to do it, least of all my husband. He's the next most experienced ringer in the band he tells me, so he'll very likely be elected Tower Captain. Then they'll all look to him to see justice is served on the murderer of their previous leader. If you don't help him, he'll go mad under the strain. Please, Mr Foxe. I'm sure they'll pay you. Captain Brock said you'd done it before, several times."

Foxe's mind was in a whirl. He'd never worked for anyone while solving crimes save Alderman Halloran. Indeed, he'd assumed hardly anyone else in Norwich would know if he'd had any role beyond being a bookseller. Now it seemed a good many knew. Brock might have mentioned Foxe's name to Mr Tate, but the suggestion hadn't come as a surprise.

They'd asked him to help them and he had no reason to say no. If he did, the whole group would be angry. Mr Tate would double the price of everything he sent to Foxe's house — as would all the others. The other ringers Mrs Tate mentioned included a fair proportion of the more successful tradesmen and shopkeepers in the city. Brock was right. He wasn't busy with anything else. Mrs Crombie ran the shop with little help from him. Lily had finished her engagement at the Norwich theatre and left to take up a new one in Bath. He was at a loose end. Far better to stop complaining and get on with it. If only Mr Tate hadn't offered him his condolences. Now Foxe wouldn't know how to dress. He might even need a complete new wardrobe.

"Very well," he said. "Please tell your husband I'll do what I can. Payment can wait until I succeed or fail. Now, is there anything else you can tell me about Mr Logan that might be useful?"

There wasn't, so Foxe headed home. He still had at least an hour before dinner. He could call into the shop and ask Mrs Crombie what kind of clothes he ought to buy.

Mrs Susannah Crombie and Miss Eleanor Benfield, her cousin and assistant, were tidying the shelves and clearing up. Piles of wrapping paper lay on the fine oval counter and there were patent medicine cabinets to be rearranged and locked. Mrs Crombie was standing on a small ladder to reach a top shelf with her back to the door. It was Miss Benfield, looking tired after her long day, who greeted Foxe first. Mrs Crombie echoed her greeting without turning around.

"Busy day?"

"Exceedingly so, Mr Foxe," Miss Benfield said. "Everyone wanted the latest gossip about poor Mr Logan." Foxe's bookshop under Mrs Crombie had become a centre for gossip. Mrs Crombie said it was excellent for trade. Those who came in only for tittle-tattle usually left with at least one purchase, hoping to prove otherwise.

"Your name was on everyone's lips," Mrs Crombie said, stepping down and turning to face Foxe. "Oh! I didn't know. Has there been a death in your family?"

It was too much. First he was called an overdressed fop, now everyone assumed he was in mourning. If that was the depth of Mrs Crombie's understanding of him, he wasn't going to ask her opinion on his new wardrobe.

"Not at all," he said, and was about to add a cutting remark when he was saved from making a fool of himself by Miss Benfield.

"Don't be silly, Cousin Susannah," she said. "That cloth is dark blue, not black. Fine material too. If you come closer you'll see I'm right."

Mrs Crombie did and agreed the colour was blue and the cloth of the very finest. Meanwhile Foxe stood like a mannequin in a tailor's shop, ignored by both of them. It was enough to make a man swear off women for ever.

At length, Miss Benfield returned to her former topic.

"We heard you have been to see Mr Tate and spent almost an hour and a half shut away with him. Half those who came here were sure it was to berate him for his high prices and poor merchandise. The rest said it was all in reaction to Mr Logan getting himself murdered. Do tell us which it was."

"Well —"

"It's obvious, Cousin Eleanor. Mr Foxe is on the trail of the killer. No doubt of it. He'd never waste time complaining in person. Plenty of grocers in the city. If one doesn't suit, you go to someone else."

"You see —"

"I suppose you're right, dear. I never bother to complain about poor service. I take my business elsewhere."

Would they never let him speak?

"You wanted to know —"

"Quite right too. It doesn't do to let a tradesman think he can keep your business whatever he does. Makes him lazy. You're like me. Won't let anyone take you for a fool."

"Ladies!"

Silence. Both turned to look at Foxe in surprise. Was he still there? How rude of him to interrupt them in that way. Surprise gave way to tightened lips and frowns of annoyance.

"You wanted to ask about my visit to Mr Tate, I believe."

Neither spoke. Their expressions did it for them.

"Well do you?"

Mrs Crombie nodded. A world of reluctant, affronted curiosity lay in that cold inclination of the head.

"I did go to see him about Mr Logan. He asked me to go. Yes, I have agreed to do what I can to see justice done. Will that content you?"

Still silence. He could talk or take himself off for all they cared. He chose the latter. As he walked towards the door into his house, he heard Mrs Crombie having the last word.

"No need to be unpleasant, was there? I expect he's upset because his lady friend has left the city."

"Probably," Miss Benfield said. "That might explain those dreary clothes too."

Foxe fled before his day was reduced to total ruin.

3

STARTING THE HUNT

Foxe was still taking his breakfast the next morning when Charlie Dillon, his young apprentice, came in with a message from Alderman Halloran. Charlie had seen Halloran's footman coming to the door and offered to take his message inside.

"The alderman requests you call on him at your earliest convenience," Charlie recited, like a child repeating his catechism. "That means come right away, Master. I expect he's mislaid one of his books again."

"It won't be that. His nieces have his library too well organised. More likely to be the murder. The alderman's a magistrate. He may even be the one who's in charge of seeing someone hang for it."

"I heard you was on to that murder," Charlie said. "Missus Crombie was telling her cousin this morning you'd solve it in no time, you being so clever and not having any distractions at present."

"Did she indeed?" He supposed Lily was the 'distraction'.

"Aye, Master. Wonderful proud of you, Missus Crombie is. Thinks you're the cat's whiskers, even if you do ..."

"Even if I do what?"

"Nothing, Master. Got to go now. She'll be wondering where I've got to."

Foxe was sure the boy was about to say 'even if you do dress like a fop.' Dammit all! Murders could wait and so could the alderman. A visit to his tailor had to be the first priority.

Like all the gentlemen of Norwich, Foxe patronised the better class of shops. They clustered along one side of the Market Place, in an area known as Gentleman's Row. There were shops all around the bustling market, but most of them still had open fronts, setting out their stock on tables jutting out onto the walkway beyond. The shops of Gentleman's Row were different. They had fine glazed windows. Their interiors were designed to suggest the exquisite taste of proprietor and customers, not do anything as coarse as promote their wares. Their customers would expect their garments to be individually tailored. They would attend the shop purely to choose fabrics and discuss their requirements with the owner. He kept illustrations of the latest fashions for them to look over.

Foxe had patronised Mr Denman's establishment for many years now and considered himself one of their most valued clients. Yet sometimes he had the sneaking suspicion Mr Denman actually judged his customers by the size of the bill he might send them each quarter. However, now was not the time for anything beyond reaching a decision on what his new wardrobe should contain. That done, he would choose fabrics and trimmings and Mr Denman would come to his house to retake his measurements.

That worthy fellow had received a new stock of cloth, so he and Foxe spent some time discussing colours and the most suitable cut for a gentleman. Foxe tried to explain he wished to be fashionable without being too outré. Mr Denman nodded in agreement.

"The word from London, Mr Foxe, is that exuberance in decoration has gone altogether too far. The latest styles are more restrained. Might I suggest a decorated and flowered waistcoat, then the coat and breeches plainer to show it off? Decorated buttons are all the rage too. The Birmingham factories produce them in metals almost indistinguishable from gold or silver. At a fraction of the price, of course. Some people are ordering their coats with as many as six or even eight buttons to each cuff."

"Very well. I'll agree to that. What should I wear on my head?"

"Wigs are smaller and simpler this season. Indeed, one or two daring fellows have even gone so far as to wear only their natural hair. It's fashionable to add a small gold cockade to a hat, I believe."

So it went on, until the intended wardrobe was complete, from hat to shoes. To the tailors unbounded joy, Foxe ordered three complete suits, plus extra pairs of breeches for each and several shirts. All to be ready as soon as possible. Since he was in a hurry, the tailor led him into a back room and retook his measurements on the spot. He promised to have the first suit ready for a fitting in a week. Foxe left feeling he had at least accomplished something that day. Mr Denman bowed him out of the shop and hurried to take the glad news to his wife.

It was high time to visit Alderman Halloran. Fortunately, it was no long distance from Gentleman's Walk to the alderman's house. You could cut through the Market Place, but something about that area always magnified the wind. On a day like today, crossing it directly would leave you chilled to the bone. Instead, Foxe stayed close in the lee of the tall buildings edging the market. Then he hastened down Exchange Street, dodged into Duke Street and crossed the River Wensum. Even so, by the time he reached Colegate Street, where the alderman had his fine house, his nose was dripping and he could scarcely feel his feet.

The alderman welcomed his visitor in his fine library. That was where he spent most of his waking hours when he could free himself from city business. He called for hot coffee, more than welcome on such a chilly day. Indeed, both men drank it standing up, their backs to the hot coals in the library fireplace. While they did so, the alderman explained his reason for asking Foxe to come.

"Wanted to talk to you about this murder of Richard Logan," he said. "Didn't know the man well myself. Very few did, so they tell me. Almost a hermit, save for his obsession with bells."

"There's no civic interest, is there?" Foxe said. "Beyond a general dislike of killings, of course."

"None at all, save that several of us are magistrates and serve in the mayor's court. It'll be up to us to hear the preliminary evidence if anyone is charged."

"General interest then."

"A little more to it than that, Foxe." The alderman left the fireplace and settled into a chair, motioning Foxe to do the same. That suggested a lengthy explanation. "Logan's father, James, was quite a famous man in his day. You'll know that. Exceptional carpenter. Designed many fine houses in the city and round about. Even made these bookshelves for my father." He waved a plump hand towards the tall racks of books on all sides.

"The city was proud of him. I recall my father telling me about some of the buildings he designed. Exceedingly proud. Logan never stood for office though. Too busy making money, I expect. Died too soon, you know, when that son of his was still learning his trade. Barely fifty, as I recall it. Terrible loss."

"But a wealthy man."

"So they said. His father and grandfather came from Scotland. They're close-mouthed about money there, I've heard. Close-fisted too. James Logan was much more interested in getting than spending. When he died, his son inherited everything."

"No wife or other children?"

"His wife had died in childbirth some ten or fifteen years before. There was a sister, but she eloped with some dashing young blade and her father cut her off. No. The son had it all."

"The business went downhill after he died, as I hear." Foxe wondered whether all this old history had a point to it.

"Yes, and quickly. Son Richard had no talent for carpentry and little business sense. He soon allowed the best work to fall away. So far as I know, all his men make now are basic window and door frames. Coffins too. That part of the business he did keep up. Richard Logan was more of an undertaker than anything else."

"What happened to the money?"

"No one knows. That's the point I'm getting at. If you believe the gossip, Richard Logan was even more careful with his money than his father was. A regular miser. Spent nothing he didn't have to, while making sure what he had would be earning more. To my certain knowledge, he owned a good many houses and tenements, especially here, over the water, where most of the weavers live."

"So ... " Fox took a few moments to think. "A wealthy man with no family. Where does his money go?"

"You've hit on it, Foxe. Where indeed? One or two of us have asked around the main lawyers in the city. They say Logan hated lawyers and would have cut off his right hand rather than pay the fees they charge. None of them admit to holding his Will."

"Perhaps it's in his house somewhere?"

"Have you been inside? I thought not. Nobody has. At least, not since his father died."

"Someone must go inside now. If there's no family to do it, someone else will have to take an inventory and see all is safe."

The alderman shifted on his chair. "That's what the mayor said. Can't leave the place abandoned. If there isn't a Will and no heirs can be found, I imagine it will revert to the crown. Anyway, the mayor wants me to do it. I thought you might agree to help me. I know it's not your affair —"

"It is," Foxe said. "George Tate spoke to me. Seems the ringers believe they're all the family Mr Logan ever had or wanted. They're going to see he's buried decently and they want me to see if I can find out who killed him."

Alderman Halloran's sigh was deep and heartfelt. "That's splendid. So you'll help me? I was almost afraid to ask. Administrative stuff didn't seem to be your kind of thing. But if you're looking for clues to his killer —"

"I'll be delighted for an excuse to look around his house, without breaking the law by doing it. When did you intend to start?"

"I thought a preliminary look tomorrow. Do you know where his keys might be?"

"If they were with his body, I expect Mr Tate has them. I'll send my manservant to ask him. Would eleven in the morning suit you?"

The two arranged that the alderman's carriage would stop to pick up Mr Foxe at his house so they could go together to Richard Logan's home. Sadly, that arrangement was destined to suffer a delay. Foxe soon learned no keys of any kind had been found on Mr Logan's body. It would need a locksmith to let them into the house and stay to open any locked places inside.

෨෦෨

FOXE SET OUT HOMEWARDS BRISKLY AFTER LEAVING ALDERMAN Halloran's house, but didn't follow his normal route. His pride was still smarting from the blows inflicted on it by Mrs Crombie the day before. If he took his accustomed route, he must pass the windows of his shop again. There he would risk encountering more locals laughing over the caricatures she'd put up. Worse, the lady herself might see him, call him inside and seize the opportunity to comment on the old brown suit he was wearing today. Thank heavens for unobservant men. He could attend on Alderman Halloran dressed in a peasant's smock and the fellow would never notice.

When he left Colegate Street, Foxe re-crossed the river and turned along Charing Cross into Upper Goat Lane. Then he braved the stench of the huge fish market and the butchers' shambles, walking along Bethel Street and around the rear of The White Swan Inn. From there, he intended to slip into his house via an alleyway that led to the back gate. He had wanted to hire a sedan chair, but there were no empty ones available. This dreadful wind would ensure the chairmen would have a profitable day.

When he reached his gate, Foxe surprised Charlie Dillon lurking there, huddled into a corner to avoid the wind.

"Gar, Master!" the urchin said, after he'd recovered from the shock of seeing his master right beside him. "What you doing round here?"

"I could ask the same of you," Foxe said. "Doesn't Mrs Crombie have any work for you? Or are you trying to slip away for some purpose of your own? Out with it, boy."

"I'm waiting for someone, like you told me to, Master. The kind of someone Missus Crombie wouldn't want in the shop." The lad had all kinds of disreputable friends amongst the street children from his days of near homelessness. They'd made him their leader, a role he still held as best he could from a secure base in his room behind Foxe's shop.

"Who is it this time?" his master asked.

"Janie. She's a whore, Master. A good one, as I'm told, though she's only fifteen or so." Foxe wondered how long it would be before Charlie tested her skills for himself. "She sent me a message she wants to tell me something about that murder the other night."

"Does she indeed? Is she reliable in what she says?"

"I reckon so. Whores always boost what they say to make it sound better, but she wouldn't dare tell me lies."

Foxe knew this was true. Charlie ruled his little flock with the severity of an oriental potentate. Lying to him would never cross the girl's mind.

"Well," he said. "Let me know what she tells you. If it's useful, there's sixpence for her. If it's very useful — and she'll tell me herself, so I can ask her questions — I'll make it a shilling."

"Hell's Teeth, Master! Add another sixpence and she'll let you fondle her titties while she talks. "

"Don't be coarse, Charlie. That's what Mrs Crombie would say."

"Aye, right enough she would. And fetch me a good clout around the ears to help me remember better. Wonderful she is."

"Go along then and wait for your friend. It's far too cold for both of you to linger out here though. Slip into the old stable. It won't be much warmer inside, but at least you'll be out of the wind. I'm away to get a glass of punch to warm me up."

"Oh ... I forgot, Master. The Captain's inside waiting for you. He talked to Missus Crombie for a few minutes then she called Alfred and he took the Captain through to wait till you came back. There's Janie now, Master. Pretty little thing, ain't she?"

She was, but Foxe knew all too well that youthful good looks soon withered in the life the girl had entered. She was also blue with the cold.

"Get her inside right away," he told Charlie. "If I remember rightly, you'll find one or two old horse blankets in the tackle room. Give her one to wrap herself in. If she wants it, let her take it with her afterwards."

As he went on towards the rear of his house, he was shaking his head.

Captain Brock explained he had come mostly to explain what he would be doing over the next few weeks. He did have some information about the murdered man, but it wasn't much. The two settled down in Foxe's library with glasses of hot punch against the cold.

"I'm not going to be able to help you as I would like this time," Brock said. "Lady Henfield has decided she wants to visit Italy on a sort of shortened Grand Tour. She's arranging to take her cousin Miss Bullen-Foster along with her, plus her maid, of course, and she wants me to go along to escort them. Got it into her head that I know how to deal with foreigners from my time in the navy. Anyhow, it's going to take a good deal of organisation and arrangement first, so I'll need to give it most of my attention. Before I get caught up in that, I thought I should do what investigating I can on this business of Logan's murder."

"Italy! Not your kind of place, I would have thought, Brock."

"Why not? Been to Leghorn quite a few times, and Rome and Naples. Sicily too. Bit fancy, I'll grant you, but still interesting. You ought to go overseas sometime, Foxe. Broaden your outlook."

"My outlook is quite broad enough, thank you. Let's leave aside your Grand Tour plans and hear what you've discovered, if anything, on the matter of the murder."

Brock glowered a little at Foxe's casual dismissal of his future journey, but settled down to explain what he'd been doing since the morning. Through a friend, who knew someone, who knew someone else, he'd got in touch with one of the bell-ringers from the tower of St. Paul's church. This was, the man said, reckoned to be the best team of ringers after St. Peter Mancroft. By their own estimation, they were the best bar none. Brock had made the mistake of asking him to explain what exactly it was that these bands of bell-ringers did.

As he related this, Brock rolled his eyes to the ceiling and let out a mighty sigh. The memory still cut deep.

"Damn me, Foxe. The fellow droned on for nigh on thirty minutes. At first I couldn't understand above half of what he said. After a while, I couldn't understand any of it and I started to lose the will to go on living."

"It's not something you'd consider as an activity for yourself?"

"I'd rather be sewn up in a sack of fresh turd and dropped in the middle of the German Ocean."

"A hard choice, I see."

"Here's the short version, so far as I could make it out."

Foxe sat back and listened. Like Brock, he had no idea what bell-ringers did beyond producing a loud noise to summon people to church or celebrate some victory. He was soon to learn he was wrong about that too.

"Bell-ringing — at least, what he said was properly called changing-ringing — is unique to England. It's a sort of team game, like cricket. You can't do it by yourself. You need at least five or six other lunatics to join in. According to him, what they do on a Sunday before services is no more than limbering up. Reminding the parson and congregation they're still about. The real stuff is different, much more serious and fiercely competitive between the better teams."

"I don't see how ringing bells can be a competition," Foxe said. "You either do it or you don't."

"That's why you and me are ignorant as pigs, Foxe, according to the greatest bore in Norfolk. I don't say I've got this completely right, but it's near enough for anyone who hasn't been driven out of his wits by the noise of his own bells."

The serious part of change-ringing, Brock said, was all about mathematical patterns. You started ringing the bells in order from the highest to the lowest. On the word of command, everyone then began shifting their bell's position in the sequence to make a fresh pattern. When each bell had rung once, they all changed again. Not randomly though. Bells are heavy, dangerous things. They can't shift more than a single place each time to make a new sequence. The aim was to run through a set number of these sequences — hundreds, even thousands of them — so you came back neatly to the highest to lowest pattern you started with. One mistake by one ringer ruined the whole thing.

"I can see it's much harder than I imagined," Foxe said. "What I can't see is why anyone would want to do it in the first place."

"No more can I. The fellow who bored me rigid about it got quite animated when I said that. He told me it was 'a unique combination of mental and physical challenges'. The ringers use their arm muscles to keep the bells ringing, either speeding their bell up or slowing it down enough to swap a position. Of course, they've also got to know exactly where they are in relation to all the others to keep in the right pattern."

"Don't they have it written down?"

"No. Couldn't read it if they did — or not in time. They have to learn it. He did show me one pattern — he called it a 'method'. Long columns of numbers, with the path of his own bell down the page marked by a red line. It looked like one of the patterns the weavers use."

"It must do." Foxe was shaking his head from side to side. An unexpected world of mathematical order and complexity had been opened up to him.

"A good number of the weavers are bell-ringers as well," Brock said. "Same trick of memory for a pattern linked to physical movements. St. Paul's is over the river on my side, as I'm sure you know. Coslany is the area where most of the weavers have lived for nearly two hundred years."

"I still don't grasp how this stuff becomes a competition."

"Each team of ringers wants to outdo the others by ringing a more complex sequence of changes or a longer one. When they do it, they have a kind of memorial board painted and set up in the ringing chamber to record the feat and who took part. They also announce it in the paper so the whole world knows."

"And the other teams?"

"Plot and practice to go one better. Either that or cry 'foul!' and claim they made a mistake or repeated some part of the sequence."

"And it can go on getting more and more complex?"

"Apparently not. There's a maximum number of unique sequences depending how many bells are involved. It's a mathematical rule and can't be broken. Even so, the potential numbers are huge, if you use enough bells. According to my informant, the shortest real peal that delivers any glory has more than five thousand changes in it."

"How on earth long would that take?"

"Three and a half hours or so. No stopping allowed."

The two men sat for a moment in awed silence.

"Not a job for elderly men then," Foxe said.

Brock sniggered. "I gather they do it sometimes. I didn't enquire about the arrangements that would likely be needed. It seems some London groups have been trying to ring all the variations in sequence possible when using seven or eight bells. That's thousands and thousands. Takes a whole day."

"Not possible, surely?"

"I don't know. You'd have to be mad, but these folks are."

"Mad enough to kill?"

"Listen to this. My chap said the band at St. Peter Mancroft were planning an especially long and complicated peal. They wanted it to be enough to prove their superiority for years to come. Richard Logan, the man who was murdered, was training the ringers. Two teams, so one could take over from the other part way through. Seems he was the only one who knew how to do it. Now he's dead, the peal's cancelled."

"Are you suggesting someone from a rival band would kill him, just to stop this peal happening?"

"Worth a thought. I tell you, these fellows are mad enough for anything — especially if there were some large bets on the outcome."

Mr Foxe stared out of the window. "Now there's something worth finding out," he said. "Yes indeed."

❧ 4 ❧

DAVY THE DIPPER

Charlie Dillon was busy. Janie's story was brief, but it could be important. Then again, it could be nothing. He was deter-mined to find out before taking it to Mr Foxe. Late that afternoon, he begged release from Mrs Crombie half an hour early on the grounds of urgent business for the master. She looked at him sharply, but let him go. It was crucial to make sure he could arrive opposite Mr Logan's house while it was still light.

Some of Logan's men were still working in the carpenter's shop by the house, but they took no notice of an apprentice wandering by. Charlie stationed himself as close as he dared to where Janie told him she had been standing. He was in a short alley almost directly across from Logan's house. It likely ran to the backs of some of the houses on this side of the street.

The wind blew down the street in piercing gusts, carrying smoke and grits from the many fires which must have been burning all that day. He could see why Janie and the other girls who plied their trade on the street chose this spot. They could step back far enough to be out of sight when it grew dark and stay sheltered from the worst of the wind. Not a comfortable place to do their business by any means, but a solid wall to lean against and firm ground underfoot. There must be a house somewhere nearby where Janie could take anyone willing to pay for greater comfort. Those too poor or mean to offer more than a shilling or two would have to make do with a few moments here.

Two market women walking by spotted the lad peering out of the entry to the alley. Their remarks showed they had no doubt why he was there. The place must have been notorious for the use street whores made of it.

"Bit young for that, ain't you boy?" one of them called. "Even if one of the light women comes along, I warrant she'll be used to stronger meat than you have on offer."

"Right enough," her companion called. "Try the molly house on the next street. Plenty there'd enjoy a fumble with young bits and pieces like yours." They laughed, their voices coarse.

Charlie was ready with a rude response, about nobody being interested in trying anything with such scraggy old meat as them, but he bit it back. They were the kind who would want to have the last word. He'd have a crowd about him if people sensed a good slanging match, preferably with some blows thrown in.

He hadn't believed Janie would tell him lies, but it was good to be sure. He imagined her standing here, letting her 'gentleman' go on his way home with a final squeeze to the front of his breeches. She must have seen anyone trying to slip into the alleyway beside Logan's house.

Before anyone asked him what his business was, Charlie darted across the street, into the alley opposite, and ran down it as fast as he could. The light was poor and he feared slipping in what felt like decades of muck piled up under his feet. If the alley where he had been before was being used as an open-air brothel, this one was the privy. His nose told him that. He hated to think what he might be treading in. He'd have to leave enough time to give his shoes a good clean before going into the kitchen for his evening meal, otherwise the smell would be enough to get him sent back outside at once.

He found the end of the passage blocked by a small shed. To the right, the wall of the adjoining house stretched the full length of the pathway, unbroken even by a window until the second storey. To the left was Logan's property. He thought its wall must be the same as the one opposite, but he was wrong. Right at the end of the alleyway, the house wall ended in a gateway that should lead to Logan's garden. The gate looked solid enough. It wasn't much more than five feet high, but it was set between brick pillars that had seen better days. The left-hand pillar in particular contained crumbled bricks that offered a foothold to the top. He bent to slip his foot into the first gap. As he did so, he could see a muddy mark left by someone else's larger foot. The mud was still damp.

Reaching the top of the gate, he looked down into a rough, disused garden full of brambles and weeds. The earlier visitor must have had a hard time to get through. Now the path he had made of broken brambles and flattened grass would be ideal for Charlie's smaller bulk. The lad found his feet just touched the ground when he hung by his hands from the top of the gate. He could avoid making a noise by jumping.

He hurried through the grass and weeds to what must be the back door. Locked, of course. Beside it was a small window. Here, Charlie struck gold. It bore clear marks where someone had forced a blade or bar alongside the window latch to make an entry. Mud on the windowsill too.

That was enough. Time to get back over the wall and make his way home before the watchmen started their rounds.

As Charlie turned around, a strong hand grasped his left arm and held him fast. Someone bent and spoke in his ear. Someone with a harsh voice and breath that smelled of onions and beer.

"What have we here? A thief and a burglar. Sneaking in, were you? Looking for easy pickings in a dead man's house. You'd be disappointed. All locked up it is. Aye, and there's an old cat and her kitten in there. One has ears sharper than any cat with fur. T'other moves almost as silently as Mistress Moggie."

Charlie struggled and kicked out, but the man was not to be shaken off.

"Come here, where it's a bit lighter. Well, well. Not one of those street brats, as I thought. Too well dressed and far too fat and sleek."

Cruel fingers pinched Charlie's stomach hard. "What are you? An apprentice run away from your master? That'll be it, I'll be bound. Good reward on offer, I imagine. Well boy, speak up! Who's your master?"

Charlie clamped his teeth together. He was sure Mr Foxe would do his best to rescue him, when he knew what had happened. Still he was damned if he was going to tell this loathsome bully anything.

"Won't speak, eh? Never mind. I'll take you along to the constable and hand you in. If there's a reward, it'll be mine. If not ... I don't like people sneaking around to steal, especially where it concerns me."

Charlie was helpless to prevent the man dragging him back to the gate. He hoped he could escape when they had to go over the top, but the man opened the gate instead and hauled Charlie through into the alleyway. By now, the boy was more angry than frightened. He should never have allowed himself to be taken by surprise. Never would have done when he was still living on his wits. The humiliation of it! To be caught by this smelly oaf and dragged off to the constable. Still, he hadn't gone inside the house, so they couldn't pin a charge of theft on him.

As he recalled the man's words, a block of ice formed in his stomach. Of course! He'd seen the window latch broken. The man had said something about everything inside being locked up and two women creeping around. He'd been inside, for sure. Had trouble escaping, by the sound of it. If he'd stolen anything, he could blame it on Charlie and see him brought up before the judges as a burglar, while he walked away, free as air.

Another burst of struggling, brought on by this realisation of the true danger he was in. It did no good. Whatever else he was, this man was strong. He also seemed to be eager that Charlie shouldn't get a good look at him. He stayed behind the boy, holding Charlie's arms behind his back, forcing him along.

Salvation came in the shape of three scruffy boys slipping in and out of the people passing along the street. As soon as he saw them, Charlie gave two piercing whistles. They stopped, stared, then disappeared.

"'Ere! What you up to?" Charlie's captor growled. "You wouldn't speak before, so keep your mouth shut now." He added a ringing blow to the back of Charlie's head to back up his demand.

The urchins were back. With them was a girl of fourteen or fifteen. She was somewhat cleaner than them, dressed in shabby finery several sizes too big for her skinny body. She walked up to the man holding Charlie, adjusted the sagging neckline of her dress to reveal a full and shapely left breast, then hitched up her skirt to give him a view of her legs.

"Fancy a feel, eh? Only a shilling. Eighteen pence for a knee-trembler in the alley over there. You won't get better."

As the man tried to push her away with a series of curses, the boys dashed in. One — Davy the Dipper — pushed a hand into the man's pocket, while the others bumped and jostled against him. Charlie knew their moves were deliberately clumsy. Davy was one of the best pickpockets in Norwich. His real victims never knew their valuables had gone until they reached for them later. The other two boys worked with him. One created a distraction and the second slipped away with whatever Davy had lifted. That way, if Davy was caught he had nothing to prove what he'd been doing.

The man felt the hand in his pocket — as they meant him to — and let out a roar of anger, trying to grab the pickpocket's arm to prevent him getting away. The slight slackening of the man's grip on Charlie was enough to let him twist out of his hands and dart off. As he looked back, he saw Davy, his skill returned, take the man's purse. One of the other lads gave the fellow a vicious kick to the shins and the second pushed him hard from behind. Still roaring, the man measured his full length in the filthy mud of the street. At that, the young whore, Janie, picked up her skirts to keep them clean and walked off. But first she stepped up to where their victim lay and kicked him hard on the side of his head. It was all over.

"Let that be a lesson to you, my boy," Foxe said when Charlie, back home safe, told him the tale. "Think before you act. If you need some sneaking around done, ask someone whose skills are still sharp enough not to get caught. I know you didn't want to come with half a story if you could avoid it, but it wasn't worth the risks you took. Still, I won't deny you've brought me the first useful pieces of information in this whole affair. Someone has already broken into Logan's house. I wonder who — and why. You say your guardian angel, Janie, says she saw someone — presumably the same man — nipping down that alleyway the night Logan was murdered?"

"That's right, Master. I didn't get a proper look at the man's face today. I could ask Janie if she thought it was the same person."

"Do so. Here." Foxe took out his purse and handed Charlie four sixpenny pieces. "Give these to your rescuers at the same time. And tell young Davy the Dipper that if he ever puts his hand in my pocket —"

"He won't, Master. They all know you — and what I'd do to anyone who tried to steal from you. Your purse is safe enough from the kids. I can't speak for the adults."

"I'm glad to hear it. Let me get this right. The fellow who grabbed you said everything in the house was locked up and there were two women prowling around there. 'An old cat and her kitten.' Servants, I expect. I was due to go there today with Alderman Halloran, but the man he sent to arrange a time came back with an odd story. The housekeeper told him most of the doors in the house were locked and Mr Logan kept the keys himself. And those keys can't be found. They weren't on the body. We assumed someone had taken them to get inside, but now that seems improbable. Why break into a house if you've already got the keys?"

"Did someone else take them, Master?"

"Two people involved in the murder, neither knowing what the other was doing? Not very likely, is it? Whoever stole the keys had to have access to Logan's body while no one else was there. I assumed that must be the murderer and he wanted to get inside the house for some reason. But if your man had to break in, he couldn't have taken the keys. That means, in all likelihood, he wasn't the murderer. So who was it?"

"It's a puzzle, sir."

"Indeed it is. Now, off to bed with you and not a word to Mrs

Crombie about your adventures. You deserve a good hiding for what you did, lad. I'll let you off this time because you've learned your lesson and you brought me useful news. Mrs Crombie wouldn't be so forgiving. You'd get a sound beating and I'd earn a lecture on the proper duties of a master towards his apprentice. Keep your mouth shut and we'll both escape punishment."

5

FEMALES OF THE SPECIES

Mr Foxe preferred to approach a new day with caution, to sidle into events as unobtrusively as he could. There was no means of knowing what might be lying in wait. It was thus his invariable habit to rise slowly, wash and dress with care, then fortify himself with a substantial breakfast. Only then would he dare to leave home to drink a cup of coffee, see what the London papers had to report and attend to any pressing business.

This was especially true when he became preoccupied with an investigation. Last night he had lain awake for a long time considering all he knew about the late Richard Logan. Even when sleep came, dreams troubled his rest. He'd woken that morning feeling that such sleep as he'd managed had done him little good.

At least a glance out of the window showed some hope of better weather. The sun was shining, though there were still a good many clouds. People weren't quite so muffled in their winter clothing. Molly had lit the fire in his dressing room. Standing in front of it and with its coals glowing, he felt quite warm for a change.

What to wear? His clothes the day before had been a little too sober. The trouble was that most of what he owned was more flamboyant than his current mood dictated. He tried to think of what might be better, but came up with a blank. He would need to ask Alfred if he could recall anything suitable.

There was no need. When Foxe went into his dressing room, he found a dark coat already laid out for him that would be perfect. When had he bought it? When had he worn it? To be honest, he couldn't remember either. Still, its dull green velvet and restrained ornament was ideal. Especially with the plain buff waistcoat and breeches his valet had set out. Buff stockings too. The man was a treasure!

Once he had dressed and gone downstairs, Foxe took even longer over his breakfast than usual. It made him late for his daily visit to the coffeehouse again, but that hardly mattered. What did cause him some irritation was noticing Mrs Crombie waiting in the hall to waylay him. She stepped forward the moment he appeared and planted herself right in his path.

"I must speak with you, Mr Foxe. Please, I must. I know you are on your way to take your coffee, but I cannot be easy in my mind until I have tried my best to explain."

"Explain what, Mrs Crombie?" His words came out even more coldly than he had intended.

"I did not intend it, I assure you. It never crossed my mind until you didn't come into the shop yesterday. Then I recalled seeing you cross the roadway when you left. Your normal habit is to look into the windows as you pass. It bothered me, so I went outside to check all was as it should be. That was when I heard them."

"Heard? What did you hear?" He knew, of course.

"People pointing and laughing at the caricatures I had set out in the window. They were saying ... they were pointing ... they assumed the pictures of the fops and macaronis referred to *you*. I wished the ground to open beneath me. You cannot know how mortified and embarrassed I felt. Had you too assumed what I had done was to poke fun at you, my greatest friend and benefactor? I rushed inside and took them down on the instant, for such an idea had never entered my head. Then, when I burst into tears and poured out my wretchedness to Cousin Eleanor, I found she had made the same assumption. That's why for the past two days you have abandoned your fine clothes.

That's why you have avoided the shop. It was all my fault, my foolishness ..."

"Calm yourself, Mrs Crombie," Foxe said. "No great harm has been done. I admit I was taken aback when I heard the comments of the crowd around the window, but I did not fasten all the blame on you. I rather blamed myself. I have been too arrogant in my desire to dress as I wish, without regard to the thoughts of others."

If that was not quite true, it would serve to avoid admitting those jibes had hurt him far more than he could have imagined.

"No, Mr Foxe. That will not do, though I know it is kindly meant. I have no right to pass any comment on your actions or choices. It is an unpardonable impertinence on my part. If I have suffered as a result, it was most deserved."

"What have you suffered, Mrs Crombie? I have neither said nor done anything."

"It is Cousin Eleanor. I told her how wretched I felt, hoping to find some comfort. Instead she said she assumed I was trying to show you how ridiculous you looked — her words, not mine. I flew into a rage and accused her of the grossest ingratitude to you and rudeness to me. We quarrelled in earnest. Cruel words were spoken on both sides. Now she says she will no longer share my lodging. She will seek rooms of her own and invite Miss Gravener to share them with her. We are barely being civil to one another this morning."

Mrs Crombie's eyes were brimming with tears as she spoke. Foxe had come to enjoy the friendly and cheerful atmosphere in the shop. If it might be destroyed, he must take action at once.

Without further ado, he waved Alfred away with the outdoor coat he had brought. Instead, he lead Mrs Crombie through the passage which passed from his house into the bookshop next door. There he found Miss Benfield and Miss Gravener whispering together. Miss Gravener he despatched upstairs to the lending library. Charlie was summoned and told to mind the shop. Foxe next pointed to the door of the stockroom and the others filed inside like prisoners going to face an especially severe judge.

For a few minutes, Foxe allowed them to stand before him, becoming more nervous as the time passed. At length he spoke.

"I have been to my tailor and ordered three new suits. All should be more appropriate to the ideas of the people of Norwich than the London fashions I have been in the habit of wearing."

Both women tried to speak, but he held up his hand for silence.

"Those are my last words on this subject. Any who raise it now will incur severe displeasure, so make up your minds to say no more about it. As for your quarrel, it arose from a misapprehension. Mrs Crombie assures me she intended no comment via the caricatures she put in the window. I believe her. What have you to say for yourself, Miss Benfield?"

There was a good deal of blushing and shifting from foot to foot before Eleanor Benfield decided the truth would be best.

"My words were ill-judged and grossly impertinent, sir. I pray you forgive me, for I repent of my foolishness. The happy, relaxed relations you have encouraged here tempted me into overstepping the bounds of familiarity. If you wish me to leave, I shall go at once, for I have no excuses."

"I do not wish anyone to leave, Miss Benfield. What I wish most of all is for things to be as they were. Will you not reconsider what I understand is your determination to leave off lodging with your cousin?"

Miss Benfield burst into tears. So sudden was her collapse and so violent her wails of misery that neither Mrs Crombie nor Mr Foxe could do more than stare at her in silence.

"Oh, Mr Foxe. You see me revealed as the wicked and heartless woman I am. I cannot bear the shame of it. What I have done is unforgiveable. Cousin Susannah will hate me and you will despise me. Oh! Oh! It is too much to bear!"

The distraught woman would have gone on like this had Mrs Crombie not swept her into her arms. She held her cousin tight, making the soothing noises you would make to a child who had fallen or taken some serious hurt. Even so, it took some minutes to restore Miss Benfield to a coherent state. Then the whole story came out.

It seemed that Miss Benfield and Miss Gravener had taken an instant liking to each other. The following weeks deepened their affection to the point where they had started planning to move in together and share their lives. All that stood in the way was Miss Benfield telling her cousin what they intended.

At this point, the malign god of false assumptions intervened. Miss Benfield convinced herself Mrs Crombie would see her departure as disloyalty. As a result, she kept putting off raising the matter, while Miss Gravener grew ever more impatient to see it done.

When the quarrel over the caricatures had arisen, much of the heat from Miss Benfield's side arose from her frustration on the other matter. Now it seemed a heaven-sent opportunity had come. She could make the break and put Mrs Crombie somehow in the wrong of it.

Of course, when she told Miss Gravener what she had done, the young woman became upset. She said it quite spoiled the pleasure of the arrangement and she would not have it begun under false pretences.

Thus Miss Benfield found herself beset from both sides. She believed she had burned her bridges with her cousin and now Miss Gravener was threatening to give up the arrangement.

Foxe forgot the whole idea of taking his morning coffee in peace. He sent Miss Benfield away to win back Miss Gravener's good opinion of her. He told Charlie to stay where he was and deal with any customers until Miss Benfield returned. Finally, he insisted on taking Mrs Crombie into his parlour and calling Molly to bring them coffee. When Mrs Crombie protested it would be quite improper for her to be alone with him, he shook his head.

"It was bound to happen sooner or later," he said. "You'll have to put up with it. In my experience, many respectable ladies flout the niceties of social etiquette as often as they wish. Indeed, not a few ignore all moral injunctions and several of the commandments on a regular basis. You're my business partner. Business will have been the subject of our discussion, if anyone asks. All I'm suggesting is drinking coffee and ironing out this silly upset. That isn't likely to offend the most maidenly of elderly aunts."

On another occasion, Mrs Crombie would have insisted on her own view of proper behaviour. Now she had spent a sleepless night cursing herself for the ingratitude to Mr Foxe and imagining his fearful anger. Taking coffee with him, even alone — save of course for a houseful of servants — was a small penance to have herself restored to his good graces. She relented and followed him into his parlour.

"Forget about those caricatures," Foxe said, after Molly had brought coffee and poured for them both. "Forget about the shop. I have more important things on my mind. Tell me all you know about Mr Richard Logan."

It was little enough. The man was a notorious recluse, Mrs Crombie said, and generally known to be a miser as well. Aside from his passion for bell-ringing, he hardly left his house. Even those who went to order a coffin found themselves dealing with his journeymen. She had used his services when her husband was taken, but never saw the owner himself. His journeyman took the order and arranged everything necessary.

"A very inferior descendent of a famous father," she concluded. "James Logan had skill and talent. His son lacked both. Some claim he's a clever man. If so, he devotes his ability only to the complexities of ringing changes on bells."

"Are people saying anything at all interesting about his death?"

"Charlie said you were involved in finding his killer, so I've kept my ears open. To tell the truth, there hasn't been much gossip at all. Of course, people are horrified that it should take place inside a church. Few have more to say. Like me, they knew nothing of him beyond his miserliness and unsociable ways."

"No one seems able to tell me anything," Foxe said. "The team of bell-ringers he led have asked for my help. They see themselves as the only family he had. Yet even they speak of him with respect rather than affection."

"People describe Mr Logan as an eccentric, but not a lovable one. It's also rumoured nobody other than his servants went inside his house. According to the more excitable, the greater part of the property is shut off and has been since the father died. They declare it's because the place is haunted."

"If every tale of haunting were proven, this city would have more ghosts than inhabitants. Superstitious nonsense! Oh it's true the house — or at least a good part of it — is locked up. Alderman Halloran and I were supposed to start today on supervising the clerks making an inventory of the house contents. It won't do to leave the place empty without knowing what's there. Do that and you make it easy for thieves to run off with who knows what and no one is the wiser. We don't even know if the man left a Will. None has been found. If he died intestate, it'll be up to the mayor, as magistrate, to arrange a search for any heirs. He'll also need to appoint executors and see to the proper disposition of Logan's estate to the crown. He's asked Alderman Halloran to oversee the start of process. Mr Halloran has requested that I help him."

"Surely the servants are still in the house. Can't they let you in?"

"Entry is not the problem. When Alderman Halloran sent a servant to a make the arrangements, an elderly housekeeper sent him back with a message. We can only enter the kitchen, dining room and her master's bedroom. For the rest, all the doors are secured and she claims to have none of those keys. She hasn't been into most of the rooms in the house since Mr Logan's father died. That was at least fifteen years ago. That's why you found me at my normal routine this morning. We've sent for a locksmith. He'll come with us tomorrow and open it all."

"If I'd been forced to wait another day to speak to you, I cannot imagine how I would have coped," Mrs Crombie said. She blinked away a few tears and sat up straighter on her chair. "Oh dear. I have yet another confession to make."

Foxe regarded her warily. When she had first entered his life, she'd been in a wretched state through the many debts her husband had left her. Foxe knew the man had been a gambler, but he hadn't guessed the extent of the losses he'd amassed. His death meant his widow was facing total ruin, maybe the workhouse. By her own account, she'd even been contemplating prostitution as the only way to survive. Foxe had given her employment, somewhere to live and a way back to self-respect and social acceptance.

Now he realised he'd grown so used to having her around he hardly looked at her any more. He knew she was a year or so younger than him and had no children. Time had also shown she possessed a willingness for hard work and a powerful business sense. They could have rescued her husband, had the man been sensible enough to realise it.

In the short time she'd been managing Foxe's bookshop, she'd transformed the place, increasing the custom and more than doubling the profits.

Now, as he watched her summoning the courage to go on, Foxe realised something else. The young widow in front of him was not only easy to talk to and well able to contribute sensible ideas. She was also remarkably pretty, in her quiet and understated way. He liked having her nearby. For a moment, he even experienced a strong urge to kiss her.

Stop! This wouldn't do, he told himself. He needed any women in his life to be carefree and heedless of the strictures of society. He wanted them to fit his fantasies, to be easy to walk away from when the time came. Mrs Crombie wasn't like that at all. She knew what constituted proper behaviour and would stick to it. She deserved to be treated seriously. Even now, she often made him face up to his responsibilities. If he became close to her, it would be worse. She might well demand actual commitment. He wasn't sure he was ready for that, now or ever.

"I'd already guessed about Cousin Eleanor and Miss Gravener," Mrs Crombie said at last. "I could hardly have missed it, the way they spoke together."

"You can tell from the manner of a conversation that two people will want to share their lodgings?" Foxe was dumbfounded.

Mrs Crombie tried to look stern, but she could not suppress her grin. "Tell me Mr. Foxe. How would you describe each of them. Be honest."

"Miss Benfield is a respectable and intelligent middle-aged lady. I would judge her to be strong, capable and —"

"And Miss Gravener?"

"Younger, of course. More uncertain in her manner. Yes, a woman who is lacking some maturity and still has to find her path in life."

"Cousin Eleanor needs to feel needed," Mrs Crombie said. "In Miss Gravener, she's found someone to mother."

"What is the problem then? Aside from leaving you alone again, it sounds an excellent arrangement."

"I don't mind being alone, though I do prefer some company in the evenings. What's making me feel bad is that I've allowed Cousin Eleanor to think she has done me wrong. I suppose I did it to punish her for setting me aside. Do you think me cruel and heartless?"

"Just human," Foxe said. "If you'll take my advice you'll say nothing. Simply show by your actions that no further problem exists. Make it clear you wish the other two ladies well, as always. If you do that, this small storm will pass soon and all will be as before."

The clock on Foxe's mantel struck noon in a pretty cascade of bells. At the sound, Mrs Crombie jumped to her feet.

"Noon already? I have been here far too long. Now my reputation will be compromised completely. You are a wicked man to detain me thus, Mr Foxe. I should never have accepted your assurances that no harm would be done. Everyone in Norwich knows of your reputation for ... um ..."

"Enjoying the company of women?"

"Enjoying it too much! Flying in the face of propriety in your ... ignoring what people ... Oh heavens! Having improper relations with a good many ladies."

"So they will assume that you and I...?"

"Mr Foxe!"

"Stay calm, my dear Mrs Crombie, I beg you. Those who wish to imagine that will already have done so. For the rest, I hardly think they will believe I have been taking advantage of you in my parlour with a house full of servants. Nor would anyone of sense imagine you would agree to behave so improperly, even if I dared suggest it. Even Captain Brock, who has known me for many years, assumes we always behave with the greatest decency towards one another. All he has ever hinted is that I ought to hurry up and ask you to marry me ..." The words were out before Foxe realised.

"Marry ... you ... marry...?

"Please, Mrs Crombie. I have embarrassed you. Ignore me. It was quite wrong of me to pass on Captain Brock's words in that way. I pray you not to let him know what I have done or he will be angry. I do apologise for my breach of decorum and good sense. Now I must let you go. Return to the shop and let your assistants see they need worry no more. It's high time I was on my way as well. I've missed my coffee, but I can still take my daily exercise."

As he called Alfred to bring his coat and hat, Foxe could still feel his face burning. What Mrs Crombie must think of him now he did not dare imagine. Why had he spoken as he had? What a mess it had made! Now, instead of reassuring Mrs Crombie that she had not upset him, he must have gravely offended her. Oh Lord, what a fool he had been!

⚮

CAPTAIN BROCK HIMSELF ARRIVED AT FOXE'S HOUSE SOON AFTER two, fortunately unaware of the ripples his casual comments were threatening to make in the relationship between Mr Foxe and Mrs Crombie. He didn't have anything fresh to report, he said. Simple curiosity occasioned the visit. He wanted to know whether Foxe had progressed any further.

The two settled in Foxe's library, shared a glass or two of good ale and talked over Logan's death yet again. Foxe brought Brock up to date with Charlie Dillon's close shave behind Logan's house. Brock pronounced himself as confused as ever.

"It's an interesting piece of news, Foxe, but it hasn't taken us much further forward, has it? All we have for certain is some unknown person hanging around the dead man's house. Did he break in? If so, what was he looking for? Money? Logan was well known to be a miser. Something else? It's an odd thief who breaks in, fails to get whatever it was he wanted and loiters around the place afterwards. If, as Charlie reports, the man said he found the doors inside locked before, does he think they may be open now? You know they are not, because you and Halloran will need to take a locksmith with you when go there tomorrow. It makes no sense."

"What kind of miser was Logan?" Foxe said. "Maybe he wasn't the type who piles up bags of coins and drools over them by candlelight. Halloran told me he believed Logan owned a good number of properties in the poorer parts of the town — and wasn't too fussy about the people he let them to either. All he cared about was having the rent paid on the dot. Maybe he used that money to buy or lease still more buildings. Could be our man thought he'd find bags of gold inside and was disappointed."

"Hard to do much with the deeds of property, even if you could steal them." Brock shrugged. "Beats me."

"It beats me too for the moment. We'll have to find out though. Knowing what the thief was looking for will go a long way to telling us who he is."

"If he was a thief."

"Charlie reported seeing the window forced and mud on the sill. Why go inside if not to steal?"

"Something to do with the bell-ringing?"

"I can't imagine what that could be, can you? Still, I suppose we ought to check the possibility. If you could have another word with —"

"No! Definitely not! Once was more than enough. If you want to know more about those cursed bells, find it out for yourself. Won't you need to talk to those who were present at the practice the night Logan died? Ask one of them. Besides, after today I really do have to turn my attention to Lady Julia's business."

The face Foxe made at this remark somehow managed to combine frustration and amusement. "Oh, very well. At least you've got a nice lady to fuss over."

"You could have one as well, Foxe. You only have to go next door to your shop."

Trust Brock to hit on the very worst topic to raise!

"Enough! I don't want to hear any more about Mrs Crombie, marriage or suchlike matters. I'm sick and tired of women and all their ways. From now on, they can all go to the devil!"

Brock stared, then burst out laughing. "Now I've heard it all! Foxe renouncing women! That's like the Pope renouncing Christianity or the French giving up wine and cheese. Dear oh dear! Who is she, Foxe? More to the point, what on earth has she done to you?"

"No one and nothing! Forget it! We've a murder to solve. Let's get back to matters of importance."

"But Foxe, this is so fascinating—"

"Not to me. Listen! We need to be certain about Logan's family, or the lack of it. Halloran said he'd speak to the churchwardens and ask to look at the parish registers. You and I, of course, know a better and much quicker way than that."

"We do?" Brock was still chuckling to himself.

"Miss Hannah and Miss Abigail. They know everything that's happened in this city over the last sixty years and more. All you need to do —"

"No! If you won't tell me about what's frightened you away from female company, I won't go visiting those two. The last time I went they knew far too much about my own business for comfort. God alone knows how they do it. Well, I guess the devil does as well. Room was full of cats. Black ones. At least three. It's not so long ago women like that would have found themselves standing on top of a large bundle of wood waiting for someone to set it alight."

"Really, Brock. Two inoffensive old ladies —"

"Inoffensive, my arse! Two of the most dangerous, scheming, nosey, evil-minded old hags you could ever meet. Do your own dirty work, Foxe. God help us, they seem to like you. 'Dear little Ashmole,' they say, 'such a spirited boy. Always up to mischief. Still, you had to forgive him, didn't you?' I don't know what you do to women, Foxe. Whatever it is, you get away with things the rest of us wouldn't even think of trying. I wouldn't be surprised if you're planning something unsuitable for poor Mrs Crombie in that evil mind of yours."

"Mrs Crombie is a most respectable lady of unimpeachable moral character."

"Up to now. Give her a few more years in your company and she'll turn into a scarlet woman."

"We seem to have returned to a topic I already told you to drop, Brock. I do not — I repeat, I do not want to talk about Mrs Crombie."

"Well I do not — I repeat, do not want to go anywhere near those dreadful old hags you term inoffensive old ladies."

Foxe regarded his friend sternly. "I do hope you didn't show such cowardice when you were fighting in His Majesty's ships, Brock."

"I tell you this, Foxe. I'd rather face a shipload of Frenchies with nothing but a rusty knife in my hand that those old women any day."

"You won't talk to the bell-ringers. You won't talk to the Misses Calderwood. What will you do, Brock?"

"Nothing. I've told you. After today I must give all my attention to Lady Julia and her trip to Italy."

"Oh, go away then. Leave me floundering. I'll have to do it all myself, as usual."

"Here's one thing I will say before I leave you to wallow in your self-pity. You've missed out at least one important source of information. Logan's workmen. What's going to happen to them? How did they feel about him? Is there someone there who might have been tempted to put an end to Logan in the hope of taking over the business for a pittance?"

"You're right. I suppose I had forgotten them. Halloran said the mayor has agreed to pay their wages from the city funds for a while. The amount spent can be claimed back from the estate when it's clear who'll get it all. I think he hopes it'll revert to the crown and he'll be able to persuade the government to hand it over to the city. That's why he wants to see the business kept as a going concern, then sold. Not collapsed and worthless."

"He might not be the only one who imagines it could soon be bought for less than it's worth."

They both sat in silence and thought about this for a while. In the end, as a final favour, Brock agreed to see what he could discover from Logan's employees. He would also speak with a lawyer he knew. From him he could enquire how long the authorities would wait in case a Will was found or an unexpected heir turned up to claim the estate. Foxe said he would try to find an explanation for the unknown burglar based on Logan's obsession with change-ringing. He would also call on Hannah and Abigail Calderwood as the best source of information on the Logan family's recent history.

"Any gossip via the book shop?" Brock asked, his voice as innocent as he could make it. "I see someone has taken down those caricatures that upset you. Shame really. Every time I went past they'd attracted quite a crowd."

"Sold," Foxe said, keeping his voice level.

"Sold? All of them?"

"All." It was an outrageous lie, but he wasn't going to be drawn back onto that topic, however hard Brock tried.

"Ordered anymore?"

"Out of print."

Brock looked at him narrowly. He must have decided that he had trespassed on this dangerous ground to the point where there might be real damage done.

"No useful gossip then?" he said.

"Nothing so far. Everyone's as puzzled as we are. They could understand Logan being struck down by an intruder in his house, attacked by a robber in the street or even poisoned by his housekeeper. To have his throat cut in the church bell tower must either be a sudden, unpremeditated act of passion or based on some logic no one can see."

"Keep digging, I suppose. Something will turn up."

"I do hope so. As it stands, we have a man killed for no reason by an unknown person in pursuit of no obvious goal. Not much of a start in solving the murder, I would say. Wouldn't you?"

❧ 6 ❧

"YOU SECRET, BLACK AND MIDNIGHT HAGS"

Next morning, the sound of muffled bells announced that Richard Logan was being laid to rest alongside his father and grandfather in the parish burial ground. Foxe considered taking the opportunity to have a word with some of the ringers, but decided against it. They might consider it in bad taste. He had no means to compel them to speak with him. Giving them an excuse not to do so seemed foolish. He would wait until Friday — their regular practice time — and try his luck then.

Foxe was due to attend on Alderman Halloran at eleven so they could leave together to supervise the inventory of Richard Logan's house. When he entered the alderman's library, he found his host in his indoor clothes and bubbling over with excitement.

"This is an odd affair and no mistake," Halloran said. "Yesterday, quite late, the mayor received a visit from a Mr Lancelot Bonnard, a young attorney newly established in practice in the city. What do you think he had with him? Richard Logan's Will, all drawn up and witnessed."

"His Will! But why had Mr Bonnard waited so long to make it known it was in his possession?"

"He's been away from Norwich visiting his family in Bungay. He didn't even know Logan was dead until he returned yesterday. Once he did, he hastened to contact the mayor."

"None of it makes sense to me." Foxe ran his hand across his brow and sighed.

"Wait until you learn what the Will contains. Logan's servants receive nothing beyond the wages owed to them. Two thirds of the rest, after payment of any outstanding debts, is to go to the United Norwich Ringers. He wants them to buy a new ring of bells for St. Peter Mancroft in his memory. One third goes to the city for a monument to James Logan."

"No relatives mentioned?"

"None whatsoever. He didn't even choose executors from friends or acquaintances. I suspect he had none. The document directs Mr Bonnard, in consultation with the mayor, to select two suitable people to act in that capacity."

"How well did Mr Bonnard know Richard Logan?"

"Never met him before he turned up at his place of business asking to have his Will drawn up and witnessed. When that was done, he asked the attorney to keep the Will in his strongroom. That was three weeks ago."

"Three weeks! My thoughts are in a whirl. It sounds as if Logan expected an attempt to be made on his life and was getting his affairs in order. Can that be so?"

"There's more. According to Mr Bonnard, all the amounts of money involved are expressed as percentages of his wealth at the time of his death. No specific amounts. There's no doubt his client was a miser. Perhaps he was a richer one than we all imagined."

"Or hoped to be. What about the properties he owned in the city?"

"None of those mentioned either. They're either imaginary or sold. How large these bequests will be, Mr Bonnard has no idea. They could be large or well short of what everyone has been expecting."

"Where's all the money? By all accounts, Logan's father was a wealthy man when he died. Since then, the word is that Logan spent as little as he could. He even shut up most of his house. At least, according to his housekeeper."

"True enough, Foxe. I'm as puzzled as you are. First the man makes a Will in a hurry, and ensures it isn't kept anywhere in his own house. The Will is also written in a way that ensures he conceals his true worth until his death. Then he gets himself murdered for no obvious reason. The mayor wants me to be one of the executors, along with yourself."

"Me? Surely not. I never even knew the man."

"Why does that matter? The mayor's view is you're already involved and acting on behalf of the principal legatees, albeit on another matter. This gives you official standing as well."

The alderman would hear no excuses. Foxe accepted the inevitable. "Are we going to start the inventory today, as planned?" he asked.

"Unfortunately not. The locksmith I hired managed to fall and break his ankle last evening. Drunk, I expect. I've found another, but he can't be available until tomorrow."

Once again, the two men agreed to meet the next morning. They would take the locksmith and a clerk provided by the mayor's office to make the inventory itself. Mr Bonnard's clerk would also be present to ensure fair play. After that they parted, Alderman Halloran went to attend a council meeting and Foxe returned home to try to make sense of it all.

One thing was obvious to him. He needed to know a great deal more about the murdered man and his history. He also wanted to avoid bumping into Mrs Crombie too soon.

That was why, half an hour later, he told Alfred to call him a chair to take him to the cottage where Hannah and Abigail Calderwood lived. He also raided Mrs Whitbread's pantry and bore off a sizeable pack of fine Bohea tea and a bottle of French brandy. He was about to confront two lionesses in their den. It would be as well to push some offerings in before him to put them in a good mood.

THE MISSES CALDERWOOD LIVED IN A TINY COTTAGE BEHIND THE cathedral. The outside was almost romantic in aspect, if you ignored the sagging thatch and marks of damp on the walls. The path to the door ran through a garden that, in summer, was a riot of colour and scents. Well, most of it was. Not far to the left of the door, a herb patch contained unidentifiable growths that looked unpleasant and smelled worse. Exactly the type of plants you might expect to provide the more venomous poisons.

Thanks to the late spring and the dampness in the air, the garden now possessed an especially malevolent aspect. The chairmen set Foxe down, took his money without comment and hurried off as if expecting to be turned into mice. Foxe noted the thin stream of smoke rising from the chimney, squared his shoulders and prepared to offer himself as a sacrifice in the cause of truth and justice.

Hannah and Abigail Calderwood were not the type of elderly ladies you 'looked in on' to lessen their loneliness with a pleasant chat over a cup of tea. Their dame school had provided a basic education to many generations of Norwich children. Most had benefitted a great deal, yet all looked back on their days there in the way slaves from the Roman galleys must have recalled their time at sea. The ladies' teaching produced brains made lean and muscular by strict discipline, constant challenges and copious hard work. Those unable to cope with this regimen, and there were many, soon begged their parents to send them somewhere else. If the request was turned down, they ran away. Those who had stayed the course now made up the majority of Norwich's most successful citizens.

Of their failures, the ladies seldom spoke, though they were not forgotten. It was common knowledge that the Calderwood sisters saw and heard everything and forgot nothing. They would look at you with kindly expressions, all the while recalling your every blunder and failing in minutest detail. If people rarely went to their cottage, it was because a visit to the Recording Angel was likely to be less painful. Judgment Day might well overlook more of what you imagined to be secret misdeeds.

The sisters also had the disconcerting habit of discussing you as if you were not present. They were doing that now with Mr Foxe. The gifts of tea and brandy had been accepted as no more than their due. Now came the consideration of the one who brought them.

"Young Ashmole always had nice manners, Abigail," Miss Hannah said. "Don't you agree?"

"Nice manners but no morals whatsoever," her sister replied. "Especially in the matter of females."

"That's true. He began so young as well. How old do you recall he was when we found him with Annie Hardacre, the Parson's daughter?"

"She was fourteen, so Ashmole must have been eleven. Mind you, she was well-developed for her age."

"They said they were playing at mothers and babies."

"I'm sure that was Ashmole's idea. Exactly the kind of devious trick he would come up with. You remember? She had him in her arms while he had his hand on one of her naked breasts and his mouth on the other."

"It was where his other hand was that concerned me. I was suspicious of that dreamy look on Annie's face from the start."

"Do you recall the time we heard splashing from the pond in the field next to the schoolroom? That was Lucy Dustan and young Ashmole."

"She said they'd fallen in. What she couldn't explain was why all her clothes had come off at the same time. Ashmole's as well. Naked as eels they were."

"It's a good job the water was so cold."

"Mary Preston was his favourite, though. Such a pretty little thing. Those enormous blue eyes made people think she was too innocent to get up to mischief. Remember when we found her sitting in Ashmole's lap and purring like a cat?"

"The time when she had her skirts spread out so carefully? I certainly do. There was a definite plopping noise when you pulled her off."

"What surprised me was how much she enjoyed being birched. Do you think that was when she decided on her future career? I gather she's in great demand. I wonder if Ashmole and she ever got together to relive happy memories?"

Foxe coughed loudly.

"Did you want something, dear?" Miss Hannah said. "You'll have to forgive two old ladies recalling a few memories. Are you still enjoying the favours of that young actress? Oh no, she's gone to Bath, hasn't she? That'll be why you're dressed like a prosperous attorney. We've noticed how the flamboyance of your clothes matches the exuberance of your night-time activities. Between ladies, then. Regaining your strength. You're not as young as you were."

"Thank God! You remember him and the time he got in through the back door of Mother Arnold's bawdy house. How many did he manage in succession? Three? Four?"

"I came to ask you for some information," Foxe said loudly. "You've had your fun. Can we please get down to business?"

"That's what he says to all his conquests, I dare say," Miss Abigail said. "We know the only business he ever has on his mind. Only we're too old."

They sighed and waited for Foxe to continue.

"I'm trying to look into some events in Norwich over the past thirty years or so."

"Richard Logan and his father. We knew them both, didn't we, Abigail. James was a most talented man. A true artist. He built the family fortune. Couldn't pass his talent on though. Richard had no gift for carpentry or business. Wonderful with figures, but quite useless with anything else."

Foxe waited. You had to let the sisters tell you in their own way. If you tried to hurry them along, or stop them wandering off into unrelated topics, they'd nod and smile and tell you nothing at all.

"Father and son were alike in one way though, weren't they?" Abigail had taken up the story. "Hard, rational men, without much sign of sentiment or emotions. Look at what happened when James's wife died. Neither father nor son ever spoke of her again."

"He never forgave the daughter too. That was something else the menfolk had in common. No one could bear a grudge like a Logan."

Foxe ventured a question. "What did the daughter do?"

"Killed her mother, didn't she? Oh, I don't mean she murdered her. She killed her by being born. Richard Logan was the couple's only child for a good many years. Then, when he was nine or ten years old, his mother fell pregnant again."

"People talked, of course. Said she'd been seeing a good deal of that wine merchant across the street, while her husband was away supervising building work. Probably nothing in it. Still, she got pregnant right enough and didn't cope with it well. The daughter was born and the mother died in the same night."

"Her father raised the child, whatever private thoughts he might have had about her origins. Never married again either. Just him, his son and his daughter in that great house. Not a man for kindness, though he knew his duty and was always fair — at least by his own standards. Stern. Strict. His word was law."

"There was one he turned to though, wasn't there. The only person who could take away the bitterness he felt towards the world, they said. The great love of the second part of his life."

"Who was that?" The words slipped out before Foxe could stop himself. He knew what the response would be.

"We won't do your work for you, Ashmole. You should know that. I expect you'll find out if you try hard enough."

He knew he would get nothing more. Better to stay silent and let them tell him whatever else they decided he ought to know.

As the years passed by, they told Foxe, James Logan's business prospered, but his family life was never more than cold. The son was a disappointment, only interested in bells and change-ringing. His father insisted he stay at home and train to take over the business, though he must have known it would be a disaster. The girl was the living image of her mother. She could have been lively and popular, if her father had not crushed her spirit. Her brother was no help either. Some elder brothers idolised baby sisters, but not him. He had as much use for her as a stray dog or cat under his feet.

The crisis came when Hester, the daughter, was eighteen. She'd grown into an elegant and attractive young woman, for all that her father denied her fine clothes or expensive jewels. He was at the peak of his fame and should have been able to give both his children a fine start in life.

"People said he was distant and prone to fancies. That's how he appeared. We knew better. Oh, he didn't drink or gamble or chase after women, and he didn't wear fine clothes. His secret was far more unusual, wasn't it, Hannah?"

"Indeed it was. I blame that earl he worked for."

Foxe tried, but he couldn't wring any more out of them.

"No, dear. We can't do everything for you, as we said. I'm sure you'll be able to work it out for yourself. Keep your eyes open when you finally get inside his house. Now, do you want to hear Hester's story or not?"

Foxe nodded and they chattered on, interrupting and correcting one another, along what seemed a haphazard path. It was nothing of the kind, of course. Foxe knew they never said anything that hadn't got some meaning attached to it. The frustration came from them forcing you to work for every morsel of understanding.

"Hester Logan grew up as unlike her brother as two siblings could be," Miss Abigail said. "Where her brother was silent and morose, she bubbled over with gaiety. He was all head. She was all heart."

Miss Hannah took up the tale. "The crisis came when her father was engaged on a complicated rebuilding project for the Earl of Brancaster. He spent weeks away, supervising work on the house and a series of temples and follies the earl wanted in the gardens."

The earl, the sisters explained, was something of an antiquarian. His particular interest was the religion of the tribes he believed had inhabited Norfolk before the coming of the Romans. His aim was to revive a proper understanding of gods lost through the spread of Christianity.

While their father was occupied with the earl's building programme, Richard was left in charge of his sister. He proved a hopeless guardian. So much so that he was taken by surprise when his sister eloped with one of the earl's nephews.

They got as far as King's Lynn where the earl's servants caught up with them. The young man imagined Hester's father would be willing to offer a generous dowry in return for a swift marriage and the avoidance of scandal. Logan refused point-blank. Then the earl added his decision that no relative of his should wed the daughter of a carpenter if he expected to have a share in the family fortune.

The nephew went to Ireland, where a more suitable marriage partner awaited him. Hester, rejected by her family and her paramour, remained in King's Lynn. Proof of the nephew's other interest in bearing her off appeared eight months later. What happened after that, the sisters didn't know. No word of mother or child reached Norwich. It was generally assumed both were dead.

By this point in the narrative, more than two hours had passed and Foxe could take no more. He made his excuses and prepared to take his leave of Miss Hannah and Miss Abigail. Naturally, they had to have the final word.

"Use your eyes in that house of Logan's," Miss Hannah called after him. "Look — and look hard. It won't have been made easy for you. Remember James Logan was one of the finest woodcarvers of his generation. That was how he expressed himself best."

"It'll be useful that he's a bookseller, won't it?" Miss Abigail added. "At least, assuming he reads what he sells. I wonder if he's ever handled any of the earl's books on Norfolk antiquities?"

"Or that place in Italy. What's it called? The one the volcano buried."

"I suppose so, dear. What could be more useful is an eye for female beauty. Don't you agree?"

"Oh yes."

"Don't let yourself be taken in by appearances, Ashmole dear. What the world is prompted to believe may not be the truth. What seems like an end may not be."

Foxe fled.

7

KILLING TIME

Foxe felt like a man who'd consumed a large, indigestible meal. What he needed now was time and space to digest it, with as plain a mental diet meanwhile as he could manage. He already had more information than he could make sense of. Yet, since he was naturally impatient, he longed to press on with his search for reasons behind the murder of Richard Logan, even though it would be counterproductive. He must wait, however much it annoyed him to do so. Tomorrow would be a busy day. First, he would accompany Alderman Halloran to Logan's house. Then, in the evening, it would be the weekly practice meeting for the bell-ringers and the best chance to find most of them together. Today was best spent letting everything sink in.

He knew if he sat at home his mind would give him no rest. Until recently, the proper course of action would have been obvious. A night of dalliance with the Catt sisters or Lily, the young actress now gone to Bath, would have offered ideal distraction for an overfilled brain. As things stood now, he had no such option.

To wander around the streets of Norwich after dusk was far too dangerous. Might there be an entertainment taking place at one of the city's halls? He could hire a chair and some link-men to light the way.

Even if he found nothing to his taste, the journey would help pass the time. If all else failed, he could swallow his pride and pay for expert hands to soothe away his worries at one of the better-class bagnios.

The hour was well advanced, so he decided to go as he was. Too late to change into anything more suitable for an evening of entertainment. He also took care to carry no more money that he judged necessary and leave his other valuables at home. He should be safe enough if he stayed in the most fashionable areas, but it would be foolish to take risks.

At first it looked as if luck had deserted him. The theatres in the centre of the city were all closed. The Assembly Rooms showed no lights or movement either. The Angel Tavern was hosting a lecture for one of the city's more sedate philosophical societies. That might send him to sleep, but was not at all what he had in mind.

Not until they had almost completed a circuit of the city centre did something catch Foxe's eye. A stream of well-dressed people moving in the direction of St. Andrew's Hall. At once he directed the chair men to follow. When they came closer, he could see a general concourse of carriages, chairs and link-men. He called to his own chair men to set down for a moment, then sent one over to find out what the event might be.

It turned out that an operatic concert was about to begin. A company of Italian singers from London had come to the city. All, so the placards declared, had trained in the finest opera houses in Umbria and the Papal States. Tonight, they were to perform a selection of arias from the works of the great Handel himself. Signor Grassini, the famous castrato, was to sing, along with Signorina Rosalba. Foxe had heard her declared a fine soprano. She was also said to be a great beauty, who had attracted the attentions of several peers of the realm.

Foxe didn't hesitate. He enjoyed music, especially the human voice. Two or three hours of world-class singing might provide the distraction he required. If it did not, there would still be time to patronise one of the bagnios.

However, he didn't need the attentions of the bagnio ladies that evening. The music held him spellbound. Grassini was the great attraction for all the women, of course, Signorina Rosalba for the men. The purity and agility of her voice were enchanting. Her talent was obvious to anyone. As for her beauty, the reports did not do her full justice. Thick, dark curls lay across her snowy shoulders and cascaded towards breasts of ravishing fullness. She made every male eye in the hall fix on her, so close was she to perfection.

When the concert ended, the rush of men towards the dressing rooms threatened to turn into a riot. Foxe turned away. There was a time when he would have joined in the mêlée, even made it to the front. Now he knew better. This would be the reaction Signorina Rosalba produced wherever she went. She would be well used to fending off the young bucks. The older, richer and more high-born gentlemen would bide their time. Their hopes to impress lay in gifts, invitations to sing at private soirées and the size of their fortunes. Foxe knew he could not compete amongst such a throng. Better to fix his aim on a more attainable young lady to warm his bed.

As he turned to find a chair to take him home, he almost collided with a late-comer to the rush. The Earl of Pentelow came striding along with all the assurance of one who knows management will clear a way between him and the target of his interest.

"Good evening, my Lord," Foxe said.

The earl hesitated a moment. He didn't want to be delayed, but the demands of good manners demanded a response. Besides, he relied on Foxe to raid his library for books whose sale might fund his gambling habit.

"Evening, Foxe. Got to rush. That fool Gosport would blather on. He could see I wanted to get away."

"Spare me one moment only, if I may ask it of you."

"Must you, Foxe? You saw her. Every fellow in the place will be around her before I can get there."

"Just one question. Have you heard of any large wagers being placed on the outcome of a peal of bells at St. Peter Mancroft?"

"What nonsense is that? Of course not. Never heard of anyone placing bets on bell-ringing. Holding me up with rubbish like ... Why? Is there a book on it? Is there money to be made?"

"Not now, my Lord. The event has been scratched. But there might have been."

"Hmm. Maybe I should ask around. Sounds foolish, but I know men who'd place bets on how many bedbugs you could find in a particular pillow. Wouldn't like to think I'd been missing out."

"Thank you. I'll not delay you further, my Lord."

"Good. Oh, Foxe. Come round to my house when you can, there's a good fellow. I'm a bit ... you know. Had a run of bad luck for a week or so. See what you can do, eh?"

"Of course, my Lord. I'll come as soon as I can."

"Capital! Right ... let's see if we can impress this Italian woman, eh? Quite a beauty. Surprised you haven't entered the race yourself, Foxe."

"I know when I'm outclassed, my Lord."

"Oh. We'll, you're right, of course. Trade can't win against birth, can it? 'Night."

Foxe stood where he was, his mind torn between pity for the countess, whose husband ignored her, and fear for the earl himself. If he did manage to become Signorina Rosalba's preferred lover for a time, Foxe was sure she would soon milk him dry. At least if the man had been single, the woman might have been held back by hopes of marriage. As it was, he could offer only rich presents in return for favours. Would Signorina Rosalba see in time how quickly these would run out? The countess's dowry was long gone, along with several of the earl's former manors. Their coffers must be as empty as their marriage.

It was high time to go home.

Next morning, a lad brought a letter from Brock. The captain had written it in haste the evening before. By now, he wrote, he would have left for London to start making the detailed arrangements for Lady Henfield's Grand Tour.

While Foxe had been visiting Miss Hannah and her sister, Brock said he had gone to Logan's workshop and talked with the two journeymen. Neither had much liking for Logan, describing him as a cold fish with no interests other than bell-ringing and money. They assured Brock the man wasn't one tenth the craftsman his father had been. The more complex commissions had ceased. Nowadays the two of them, with two half-hearted apprentices supplied by the Overseers of the Poor, handled all the work with time to spare. Brock wrote neither had struck him as a hard worker either. He wasn't sure they were even competent carpenters. They had an easy life and a master who rarely came to see what they were doing.

Foxe sat back to think about this. Was Logan making a large enough income to cover their wages? The next part of Brock's letter answered his question.

Encouraged by the brandy Brock had brought along, the journeymen soon forgot to watch their tongues. Logan cheated his customers, they boasted, especially over coffins. They helped him do it. Logan had shown them various ways to make cheap materials look like expensive ones. They would urge grieving relatives, especially widows, to give the loved one "a proper coffin that will last in the earth". Then they would make the coffin from cheap deal planks, stain it with certain dyes and polish it with beeswax and turpentine. The result, to an untrained eye, was a good approximation to oak. Once in the ground it would rot within months, but no one would see. Logan also paid certain sextons to remove brass coffin handles and fitments, returning them to him for resale and reuse.

All very unpleasant and disreputable, Brock concluded, but hardly a motive for murder. He had hoped to find something more heinous than cheating the customers.

Foxe sighed and folded the letter. With Brock gone, he felt very much on his own. He relied on their conversations to help him set his own ideas in order. Who would do that for him now?

Foxe reached for the nearest coffee pot and found it empty. Good Lord! He'd emptied both pots already. He'd be awash with the stuff. Now even the thought of going to the coffeehouse made him feel nauseous. What to do instead? His clock chimed. Ten o'clock. The alderman's coach was to pick him up at noon. He glanced out of the window. Rain. Walking around the Market Place was out of the question.

The obvious way to spend the time was to go into the shop. He'd not been there for almost two days now. If only it hadn't been for his foolishness in letting slip that remark about asking Mrs Crombie to marry him. She was a level-headed woman, but what if she'd taken his words seriously? Might she have assumed it was a roundabout way of making a proposal? At the time, he'd escaped before giving her any chance to respond. He thought he'd been clever. Now he was far from sure.

The trouble was he didn't know himself what his feelings about marriage were. It was something other people did, not him. Yet look at him now. Lonely. Reduced to considering paying for female company, something he hadn't done for years. Times were changing. Even the actresses at the theatre weren't as eager for dalliances with older men as they had been. Damn it all! Some of them believed they could forge themselves a starring status through their talent alone.

There must be many widows in the city who might be grateful for his attention. Would any of them be as clever and thoughtful and ... well, attractive ... as Mrs Crombie? She was rather proper, but he felt sure he could tempt her out of that. If only she weren't quite so competent, so willing to take charge. Young Charlie worshipped the ground she walked on. The fact that she spent a good deal of her time trying to eradicate the street-urchin in him didn't seem to bother him at all. Would she do the same with Foxe, given a chance? Would the price of loving companionship be accepting reform?

He looked across as the clock. Five past ten. Five minutes wasted in fruitless speculation and avoiding the issue.

Foxe rose, stood for a moment looking out at the rain, then made his decision. He would face his fears this time, not run away. As he walked through the hall and down the passageway to his shop, he bore the expression of a Roman gladiator going out to meet his fate in the arena.

He'd hoped there would be customers, so he could dispense suitable greetings and slip away again, but luck was not on his side. The place was empty, save for Mrs Crombie, Miss Benfield and Charlie. The lad was sweeping, a job often assigned to him, but one he seemed to relish. Miss Benfield had her back to the door through which Foxe entered. It looked as if she was tidying some of the patent medicines they sold in surprising large amounts. Mrs Crombie was standing behind the counter.

"Good morning, Mr Foxe," she said as he came in. "I hope you are well. Business is slack today, as you see. One or two ladies are upstairs in the lending library, but otherwise the rain has kept most people at home."

"Quite well, thank you," Foxe said, relieved at her matter-of-fact tone. The others echoed her greeting. Miss Benfield returned at once to her task. Foxe was sure it was to avoid any questions about Miss Gravener. Charlie put his broom down and came over to listen. His curiosity was as shameless as Foxe's own.

"I'll be going to Mr Logan's house with Alderman Halloran later this morning. The mayor has asked us to start on the probate inventory."

"Please let us know if you find anything unusual. We've all been encouraging the customers to gossip, but there's been hardly anything of value. How did your visit to the Misses Calderwood proceed yesterday?"

"Much as you would expect, I imagine, if you knew them."

"Everyone knows them, just as they know everyone. My late husband attended their school and it left him with a deep aversion to learning for the rest of his life. I suspect he wasn't an ideal pupil. Too restless to pay attention to anything for more than a few moments at a time. Still, what they recommend — if they recommend anything — is always well worth considering."

"They told me that when I get inside the house I'm to use my eyes and remember Logan's father was a woodcarver. They also implied the man had some secret indulgence."

"I might be able to help you there. My own father was a great admirer of anyone who helped uncover Norfolk's past. Did you ever hear of the Earl of Brancaster?"

"Vaguely. Rich and eccentric, as I recall. Got some bee in his bonnet about ancient mysteries. I recall he wrote a book about it and sent copies to learned societies and unwary friends."

"That is so. He also employed James Logan a good deal. They became quite friendly, especially after the earl decided to have a range of temples constructed on his estate."

"Temples?"

"Most people assumed they were follies or garden ornaments, but my father never agreed. The book the earl wrote was a serious attempt to uncover the religious beliefs of the pre-Roman tribes in this area, he said. Those buildings may or may not have been intended for any religious use. He still believed the earl and Mr Logan were trying to recreate the design and contents of genuine Druid temples."

"Hmm. No one has suggested Logan's son shared his curiosity in such matters. Up to now, there's not been a hint of anything that could lead to murder. Miserliness, dishonesty, an obsession with bells. None of it suggests the kind of hatred, fear or jealousy that leads someone to commit murder. No one kills because of their views on dead heathen practices."

"Greed?"

"I suppose I may get some idea from what's in that house. The lawyer who drew up Logan's Will said the properties the dead man was rumoured to own were either sold or an illusion. People saw a miser and assumed he must be rich. Maybe even his father wasn't as wealthy as people believed."

"That could be. Don't dismiss what Miss Abigail and Miss Hannah told you though. I've heard they never say anything without a good reason."

"Are they really witches?" Charlie's eyes glowed with excitement.

"No, lad. Just two elderly ladies who take advantage of their age to speak and behave outrageously. They used to run a dame school and so got to know a good many people in this city. Being almost as curious as you are, they found out everything they could and remembered it all."

"Do they have a cat?"

"Several, I believe, though I didn't see any yesterday."

"Black ones?"

"I think so."

"Then they must be witches. Witches always have black cats. At least, they do in the tales Missus Crombie is teaching me to read. I'd like a cat. Do you think they'd give me one of theirs?"

"It's not nice to say an old woman is a witch, Charlie," Mrs Crombie said. "People used to be afraid of witches and believe they could cast spells and lay curses. They persecuted them and burned them alive because of it. Witchcraft is one of those dead, heathen practices Mr Foxe says no one ever killed for."

"But you just said ..."

"Mrs Crombie is quite right," Foxe said. "I should have known better than to make light of what she was telling me. Remember that, lad. Always pay close attention to what Mrs Crombie says to you. She could even be a wise woman herself."

"A wise woman? Is that something special?"

"Isn't it time you were on your way, Mr Foxe, before you trespass on my indulgence too far?" Mrs Crombie said. "I can see I need to take you in hand, in case you undo all my efforts with this young man."

"But—"

"Alderman Halloran won't like to be kept waiting."

Foxe endeavoured to smile, but her words sounded ominous. Wasn't taking you in hand what a wife tried to do?

8

INSIDE THE HOUSE

By the time the alderman's coach drew up outside Foxe's house, the rain had stopped, though the clouds remained low and threatening. Servants out on errands splashed through the mire. One or two skidded and slipped on the mess beneath their feet. The rain hadn't been hard enough to wash much into the few drainage runnels, so the combined filth of mud and household waste was undiminished. Foxe was glad to be travelling by coach. He hated the sensation of slime under his shoes and mud splashing up his calves. As they went the short distance to their destination, he noted that most of the quality must feel as he did. Few were about, save one or two ladies struggling along wearing pattens to keep them out of the mud. They were probably making late calls on their acquaintances.

Logan's house lay in an area of the city which had once been prosperous, but was now sinking into neglect. Foxe judged it must date from a good many years ago. The neat, brick and stone frontage and fine sash windows onto the street might fool a few passers-by. Yet if you glanced down the alleyway between it and its neighbour, you could see the bulk of the fabric was framed in wood. Many house owners retained a sound Elizabethan structure while giving the building a modern face.

They knocked at the door and were greeted by the housekeeper. She introduced herself as Mrs Baker. A slim woman, well-dressed in dark worsted cloth and with a lace cap to cover the mass of grey hair about her head. A little past middle age, Foxe thought. Anything from her early fifties to sixty or so. He assumed she had been the father's housekeeper and stayed on to serve the son.

Closing the door, she led them through an arch into a good-sized hall. It had lost the gallery that must once have stood at one end, but retained the rich oak panelling on the lower half of the walls. A great table filled the centre of this space, so large it may well have been built where it stood. Ten chairs, seats and backrests upholstered in dark red brocade, were set in two groups against the wall opposite the street. Between the groups, a fireplace of pale stone, topped by a carved coat of arms and crest. All around were what appeared to be family portraits. It was in every way the type of home you would imagine belonged to a long-established family of merchants or manufacturers.

The only jarring note was a small card table, with a single chair, set in a corner away from the windows. An upholstered sofa stood close beside it. This, the housekeeper explained, was where the master had taken his meals and rested afterwards with a book or his writing materials. The great table had not been used since the old master died. All the silverware, glasses and china were in what had been the butler's pantry. None of it was new and a good deal of the china was chipped. She did her best to keep it clean, but the master regarded it with little interest.

"Did he not entertain?" Foxe asked.

"Never once since his father died," the housekeeper said. "He did not keep a cook either. I cooked for him. His wishes in that regard were few and plain."

"And you cleaned the house too? Are there no other servants?"

"A maid, sir. We share the work between us, for it is little enough. Aside from spending time here, the master used only his study and a dressing room and bedroom on the floor above. All the other doors outside the kitchen and domestic areas are kept locked. I have my own small room close to the kitchen. The maid, Jane, no longer uses the bedrooms in the garret. It's a long way from here and she felt nervous about being up there on her own. I converted the old stillroom into a bedroom for her. We two take our meals together in the servants' hall, though it's far larger than we need."

Alderman Halloran told the locksmith he could leave them and begin work on opening the locked rooms. He also waved away an invitation to inspect the kitchen and other domestic offices. Instead, he walked back past the front door into a room furnished as a small parlour. Most was covered with dust sheets. There was another door opposite the front entrance, but that was locked.

"Where's the staircase?" he asked the housekeeper. She led them through a door at the far right of the hall to a narrow, dark stairwell. The staircase was made of oak. Its carved newel-posts and balusters showed it too dated from the time the house was first built.

"That leads up to the master's rooms," Mrs Baker said. "There are other bedrooms on that floor too, in two short wings. They're all locked, as I told you. There's also a library above the hall itself."

"Locked?"

She inclined her head in agreement. Standing there, she seemed somehow more the mistress of the house than a servant. There was something calm and authoritative in her manner of speaking. It did not fit a mere housekeeper, however long she had served the family.

Alderman Halloran went up the stairs, beckoning Foxe to follow him. At the top, they found a locked door to their left — doubtless the library. Another door opened into a wing of the house stretching away from the street. Foxe guessed the servant's hall, stillroom, scullery and pantry must be on the ground floor of this wing, with the kitchen projecting beyond.

Opening the door, they found themselves in Logan's rooms. The alderman turned to Foxe at once.

"What do you make of it? I don't know what I expected, but not a mansion like this. Even if it does date from two hundred years or so ago, it's a substantial property. Very much a gentleman's house. Why confine yourself to a few rooms and lock all the others?"

"I have no idea," Foxe said, "Logan never entertained, it seems, nor welcomed visitors. He used what he needed and gave no thought to the rest. A recluse, as people said. Living that way also meant he needed but two servants, so less cost as well."

"I don't know, Foxe. It's not the way any sane man would choose to live, is it?"

"No one has suggested he'd lost his wits. This is the dressing room, with a clothes press, two hard chairs and a small table. He didn't do anything here but dress himself. A long glass — somewhat misted — a wig-mirror and some small brushes. I don't like the pale green walls, do you? Cheap prints instead of pictures. A turkey carpet on the floor. Even that isn't of much quality. It must have been here for years. See here ... and here ... and here too. A good many signs of age and wear. This corner looks to have been chewed by the mice."

"Perhaps his bedroom will tell us more."

It did not. There were windows with wooden mullions, as you would expect in a house of such age. Small, diamond-shaped panes of glass with lead between them. On a day like today, they let in a dim light that was just enough to see by. Such furniture as there was seemed of good quality, though old-fashioned in style. A bed with a plain tester and dingy curtains. One or two gloomy oil paintings. Several pieces of good china on the mantelpiece. An anonymous place that could have been a guest bedroom for all the signs it bore of anyone's personality.

"Not a personal room, is it?" Alderman Halloran said. "Somewhere suitable for a single necessary function, otherwise ignored."

Foxe said nothing. Something about the place was starting to make him feel uneasy.

Hearing the locksmith coming up the stairs, they went back onto the landing. The man confirmed that the other doors downstairs were now open. Foxe asked him if he could tell how long the doors had been locked.

"Not that long, most of them," the locksmith said. "A bit stiff, but none were hard to unlock. No rusty locks or hinges. A few years at most, maybe less. All but one, that is. There's a door that opens into a small room off the parlour. That's been kept well oiled. There's a desk there, so I suppose the owner used it as a study. I'll get on, shall I?"

"Open this library door first," Alderman Halloran said. "Then you can deal with the others."

They left him to his task and went back downstairs. Alderman Halloran busied himself about the hall, inspecting the furniture and paintings and opening one or two cabinets. Foxe still couldn't shake off the sense of there being something wrong. He looked around him, yet failed to discover what might be making the hairs on the back of his neck bristle as they did. Everything bore witness to a house that had once been magnificent, filled with items of the best quality. Yes, there were signs of neglect. The carpets were dusty. They could not have been lifted and beaten for years. Spiders had spun their webs everywhere a person standing with a duster could not reach. There was a slight but pervasive smell of mouse urine.

What wasn't right? Why did he feel he was missing something important?

They went into the small room off the parlour. Despite the locksmith's observation that someone kept the lock oiled, there was dust here as well — on every surface save that of the desk. That must have been in regular use. Somehow it looked too big for this room, as if it had been brought from elsewhere for a definite purpose.

Foxe glanced down at the carpet and touched Alderman Halloran on the arm.

"Look, Alderman. The carpet hasn't been cleaned properly in ages. Not even swept, I would say. Someone's left a pathway though the dust heading over there. Let's see where it leads."

It took them across the room to where a tall screen stood, shutting off one corner. Halloran paused to examine it.

"Fine screen this, Foxe. Came from China I should say. It's covered with pictures done in the kind of coloured lacquer they use there." He touched it and pulled his hand back with a grunt. "Covered with dust, too."

"But what is it hiding?" Foxe managed to slither between the screen and wall behind without getting too coated in grime.

"Look at this, sir," he said. "What do you make of it? Iron and octagonal, with heavy hinges to a flap on the top and two keyholes."

"By God, Foxe. That's as strong a document safe as I've ever seen. You'd never move it. Far too heavy. See if it's locked."

"Locked tight. We'll need to ask our locksmith, but my guess is this was made to be proof against most efforts to find a way inside — unless you have the keys."

The locksmith, summoned back downstairs, shook his head and agreed with Foxe. "I don't think I've ever seen such a large lockbox before, sir. Cast iron, I would say, several inches thick. If you look at the keyholes, you can't see any sign of the lock mechanisms. It will need keys with mighty long shanks, so the locks would be impossible to open with picklocks. Either the picklocks wouldn't reach or they'd bend before they could shift the wards enough. Whoever made this knew what he was about. You might be able to smash the lid in with a hammer and a cold chisel, but I wouldn't even be sure of that. It's beyond my skill to open, Masters. Of that I'm sure."

Foxe looked at the safe with loathing. "Whatever is in there was judged important enough for the most extreme measures, Alderman. I wish I could guess what it was. Money? Papers? What?"

"Even if you filled it with bags of gold sovereigns, it isn't large enough to contain more than, say, five or six thousand pounds. A goodly sum, but not a king's ransom. I can't make head nor tail of it either. What papers could be so secret you'd lock them up like that, save in the royal palace? The man was a local carpenter, Foxe. He wasn't a minister of the crown or a foreign envoy."

Odd. Damned odd. Its presence jarred on Foxe, like almost everything else in this house. Why put a safe like that in this room? Shouldn't it be in an agent's office or somewhere, not in this domestic setting?

After a while, they gave up on the puzzle and returned upstairs to see what else they might find. At the top of the stairs, they met Mr Bonnard, the young attorney.

"Two bedrooms in the right-hand wing, gentlemen, one with a dressing room, and another one over the parlour. All full of dust and damp. The only other room is the library. The locksmith's opened the door, but it's too dark inside today to see much. All I could make out were a table, a few chairs, two globes and shelves of books. We'll rely on you for a valuation there, Mr Foxe."

Foxe and Halloran perked up at the prospect of a room full of books untouched for twenty years or more. They sent the locksmith up to the garrets and hurried to look at what might be in the bookcases.

It turned out to be something of a disappointment. A dozen book-presses with eight or ten shelves each. Foxe scanned the spines of the volumes on some of the lower shelves. He straightened up with a sigh of frustration.

"An odd mixture in these two," he said. "Rows of dull-looking books of Biblical commentary and sermons. The usual copies of Latin and Greek texts. Apart from those, some volumes of architectural drawings and carvings. All standard fare. Palladio, that kind of thing. Might have a modest value, provided they're not riddled with damp and bookworm. Nothing rare that I could see."

"Same in this one, along with some books of mathematical theories. What do you think? Forty to fifty years old, most of them? More? I'd say these were more for show than for use."

"Great heavens! I was so keen to look for rare books I ignored the book-presses," Foxe said. "Have you ever seen any before with so much carving on every surface? Look at all that openwork along the top and the sides. Leaves, tendrils, odd faces, birds, every possible decorative device. I know the father was a famous woodcarver, but this is quite amazing."

"Look at this library table, Foxe. Carving around the edge, as well as on the pedestal it stands on. Even the table top is covered with a mass of carved wood inlay — where you can see it through the dust."

"At least the panels on the wall are more restrained. Hold on though. What's this? I thought it was a simple moulding around the edge. It's a thick rope, carved in wood, with faces and flowers and odd hands and toes peeping out from it." Foxe ran his fingers along the wood, feeling the depth of the undercutting.

"Beats me why he did it, Foxe. Perhaps he was bored with the tasteful, restrained work he had to do for his clients. Wanted to keep up his skills by using his house as a kind of exercise ground."

"It's much too dark in here to see all this work properly, Alderman. Can you open some of the shutters? They must have been closed to stop the light fading the spines of the books. That's better. My God!"

"What is it, Foxe?"

"Look at the figures in the panelling. Gods, goddesses, snakes ..."

"Are you serious?"

"I most certainly am serious. I missed seeing them at first because it was so dark in here. They're dusty and covered with cobwebs too. This is work of breathtaking skill."

The alderman came to stand next to Foxe and peered at the figures.

"Am I seeing what I think I am, Foxe? Look here. I know it's conventional to depict gods and the like naked, but is it usual for their ... um ... private parts ... to be depicted so clearly?"

"Certainly not if they're as erect as that one is. Look at the nymph, or whatever she is, with him. I think you would describe her genital area as depicted in loving detail."

"Pornographic, I call it," the alderman huffed, but Foxe had moved on.

"Same on this panel," he called back. "Sea monsters, mermaids, great fishes. What's this mermaid holding? Ah, no wonder the merman looks so happy with life."

Alderman Halloran had drawn back from the panelling and walked over to two large globes standing by the far wall. On a narrow table between them, he'd spotted what he thought might be a copy in bronze of some famous Classical sculpture. He had two or three in his own home and was quite proud of them.

As he got closer he hesitated.

"Foxe!" he called out. "Come here. What on earth is this? I assumed it must be one of those satyrs from Greek legend. The ones with the head, arms and body of a man and the legs of a goat. But it's not like most of the examples I've seen."

Foxe walked over, bent forward and began to chuckle. "His horns are far too big for any goat. More like the curled horns on a ram. The woman he's ... about to enjoy isn't a classical nymph either. Too lush about the breasts and too obviously female. Still, by the expression on her face, she's expecting to have a fine old time of it. Have you seen the size of his male member?"

"Disgusting, I call it! Disgusting!" Alderman Halloran took a careful look anyway. "We ought to throw a cloth over it. It's indecent. There are women in this house."

"We'll get the locksmith to lock this room up again, shall we? Let's close the shutters again too. You know, Mr Bonnard came in here and never mentioned this. Either he's quite broad-minded or he didn't look about him very well."

"We didn't see any of it while the shutters were closed."

"True. It's very cleverly done. Unless you take a close look you'd assume it's a bronze copy of some Greek statue of Silenus with a nymph. Mildly shocking, but hardly unusual in a gentleman's library. Most would have some suitable drapery hiding their private parts. This one hasn't, but you have to come close to see the truth of what's going on."

"French, I imagine."

"Given the skills of the former owner of this library, I'd say it was most likely made in Norwich. Did he have a salacious streak, I wonder? Was there some other message? Mrs Crombie told me he worked a good deal for the Earl of Brancaster. I gather he was a noted antiquarian with an interest in the religions of pre-Roman Britain."

"Let's go, Foxe. Forget that regrettable sculpture. There's nothing of great value in the house."

"Unless it's in that safe."

"Indeed. But no one is going to get to it there. We can ask Mr Bonnard to get his clerk going on the detailed work now. Better warn him about the statue. Ask him to cover it up and tell the clerk you'll make a suitable valuation later. Come back another day to look at the books too."

"You know, Alderman. Most of what we've seen in this house has made me distinctly uneasy. It's more than neglect. Rejection? Antagonism? I don't know. Yet this room is quite different. It may be odd, but it's full of life and laughter and joy somehow. Don't you feel it?"

"I do not. We all know your reputation, Foxe."

"Oh, come now, Alderman. Was there never a time in your youth when you wanted to get up to things that would scandalise your parents' generation? Did you never look at a pretty girl and find certain thoughts and images running around in your head?"

"Well ... maybe, I suppose. But now I know better — and so should you. Come along. We came here for a serious purpose, not to rekindle the errors of our youth."

ૹ 9 ૠ

CHANGING COURSE

Foxe called into his shop on his return from Richard Logan's house and found Charlie waiting for him in a ferment of excitement. Mrs Crombie could do no more than smile a greeting before Charlie hustled Foxe into the stockroom away from listening ears.

At his master's request, the lad had organised the street children to watch Logan's house. They took it in turns, begging or playing in the roadway during the day and huddling in a group after dark. Despite the pennies Charlie brought them, one or two of the older girls had been seeking custom from the men passing by. Any fleeting visits to various alleys to ply their trade didn't stop them from keeping their eyes open, they said. Some of the boys also picked pockets, but Charlie took care not to mention this.

Janie had come about an hour earlier and brought Charlie a report.

"That man's been back both nights, she told me," Charlie told his master. "Keeps away during the day. They think he's trying to find a way inside, but all the shutters on the windows are closed — probably barred too. Someone's blocked the small window he used before."

"Tell the children they've done well," Foxe said, "and to keep it up.

Now they've seen him on two occasions — and for longer — can they describe him in any detail?"

"You gotta remember he only comes at night, Master. Hard to get a good look. One of the girls went up to him in the way of trade, as it were. She says he's not too old — the same age as you or a little younger. Dresses like a fisherman or sailor, she told Janie. Skin's all weathered and tanned as well. He pushed her away. Quite rough he was too."

"That's something to start with. If he's anything to do with the sea, he'll have come here from Yarmouth or Lowestoft. Here's what to tell them. Stop watching the house and watch this fellow instead. Find where he's staying in the city and what he does all day. Is he visiting several houses with a view to burglary? If he is, I doubt he'll be of much interest to me. If Logan's house is the only one that he goes to, I need to know as much about him as possible. Tell them not to let him suspect he's being watched. I want him to keep trying to do whatever is on his mind. If he isn't local, he'll need to pay for his bed and board. The longer he must stay here, the more desperate he'll become. Desperate people take chances that lead to mistakes. Do you under-stand what you have to tell them?"

Charlie nodded.

"Very well. Another penny a day each in view of the extra work. Off you go! If he comes again tonight, they should stick to him and see where he goes to sleep."

Charlie ran off, his head full of his master's directions and cautions to the children.

When Foxe returned to the shop, Mrs Crombie was waiting for him.

"I hope you're not putting those children into danger. It's all very well giving them a few pence. What they need are homes and good food."

"Those things are beyond my power to give," Foxe said. "Where would I find people to take them in? Most of them ran away from homes — of a kind. Regular food too, if not food much worth eating. I'd take a large wager that more than half come from orphanages or apprenticeships arranged by the Overseers of the Poor. The rest ran away from home. They see most adults as the enemy, Mrs Crombie. That's why they rely on one another. I can't change that, but I can try to make sure they have the few pennies they need to buy something to eat."

Mrs Crombie sighed. It was clear to Foxe she knew he was right. What pained her was the wretchedness of the world and the plight it too often forced on young and old alike.

"You have a kind heart, Mrs Crombie," Foxe said.

"A soft head, too," she replied. "There are times when I wonder if goodness itself is any more than wishful thinking."

"Cheer up! Charlie is on the way to a far better future than a year ago. Who knows? Maybe by showing these other children there are adults who won't exploit them we can restore a little of their trust in people generally. Now, how has business been today?"

As Mrs Crombie detailed the day's takings and orders, her spirits rose again. Business was good, both in books, the library and sales of patent medicines.

"Any useful gossip?"

"Before we talk of that, Mr Foxe, may we go where we can speak in private? I will come through into your house on this occasion, if you wish it."

Foxe's heart sank. He'd hoped she had forgotten his careless remark or decided to ignore it. He led the way into his parlour, as before. Mrs Crombie refused coffee or any other refreshment. She also remained standing, despite his suggestion that she would be more comfortable if she sat down.

"This will not take a moment," she began. "I am sure you did not mean to make the remark you did about Captain Brock urging you to make me a proposal of marriage. Such a thing may be far from your mind. Even so, the idea was raised and I believe it would be dishonest of me to ignore it."

Foxe said nothing. Better let her speak her piece, then choose how to respond.

"I have thought a good deal about my future, Mr Foxe. I am very happy here and believe my life is set on a sound course, thanks to you. I will not say that the notion of marrying again has not occurred to me. Nor will I deny that it has its attractions. I am still of marriageable age and do not believe my person to be wholly unattractive. However ..."

She paused, gathering her courage for the main point of what she wanted to say.

"... a general consideration of marriage is one thing. An actual proposal from a specific person is quite another, especially if you were that person. I will not marry from gratitude, sir. Nor will I set propriety so high as to accept a proposal to satisfy social conventions. Yet what would weigh most with me is your indecision about your own future. I do not believe you know what you want, Mr Foxe. You are fickle and prone to following fashion. You make sudden changes of direction, thrusting the past aside and rushing headlong in a new direction. For example, because of some small irritation with public comment, you abandoned the style of dress you spent so much on until now. You have, as it seems to me, lost your interest in buying and selling rare volumes. You leave the operation of the shop to me. Even in your investigation of this murder, you seem to have no plan. Instead, you respond to whatever information comes your way. You jump from idea to idea where you should be following a logical path.

"Find yourself a purpose in life, sir, instead of flitting from pleasure to pleasure like a bee tasting flowers. Until you do, no woman worthy of you will take a marriage proposal seriously. What she accepted today might be different tomorrow. When you are sure what you want of a wife, you may, if you wish, approach me at that time. Then — and only then — I will consider what you ask and give you my answer.

"Now, let us turn to other things and say no more on this topic. I will return to the shop. If you wish to discover what gossip has reached us about Mr Logan, come through when you are ready and I will tell you."

Foxe was too surprised to speak. He had feared either a blunt refusal or an eager acceptance, not this analysis of his behaviour. Part of him wished to take refuge in anger at the woman's presumption. Unfortunately, the greater part knew she was right. He didn't know what to do with himself. He had no specific plans or intentions. Much of what he did he chose on the spur of the moment, relying on his wealth to save him if it went wrong.

She was also correct about this investigation. He had accepted the request to probe Logan's death as much to ward off boredom as from any concern for finding a murderer. Since then, his actions could be summed up as following the most obvious path and taking advantage of luck. Without Brock to test his ideas and keep him up to the mark, he was collecting information in the hope something would turn up — yet he didn't know what.

Mrs Crombie's words were all too true. That dandyish image and careless disregard of social conventions helped him avoid responsibility. His many affairs with women were confined to those not seeking long-term commitment. In a young man, such a style of life would produce no more than wry acceptance — the usual sowing of wild oats. In a man of thirty, like himself, it had become unfitting. If he persisted with it as he grew older, the people he most associated with, those solid burghers of Norwich, would despise him.

It was time to set youth aside and behave like an adult. There could be no running away. He would solve this murder by using his brain and following a proper plan. Once that was done, he would choose a proper path through life. If that needed a different relationship with Mrs Crombie, Charlie or anyone else, so be it. In the meantime, he was hungry and it was almost time for dinner. No, before then though he needed to salvage a little of his pride by going into the shop and acting normally. Afterwards, he could eat.

Mrs Crombie's collection of gossip wasn't large, nor was it as surprising as it might have been, given what Foxe and Alderman Halloran had discovered in the library of Logan's house. The latest notion going the rounds was that the ringing of the church bells was disturbing a local coven of witches. Bells were said to be hateful to demons. Whenever they rang, the witches were deprived of their familiars. Then they were powerless to pronounce curses, summon up storms and generally blight whatever was good and wholesome. Driven to desperate measures, the gossip went, they had summoned Beelzebub himself and sent him to cut Logan's throat.

All nonsense, of course, but it might link back to some half-forgotten memory of the Earl of Brancaster's interests. Did people also recall James Logan's involvement in designing 'pagan temples' for the earl's estate. How could he find out?

Of course! The Earl of Pentelow wanted him to find buyers for more of his books to fund his gambling. Pentelow's father had been a noted collector, as well as an amateur antiquarian. He must also have been a contemporary of the Earl of Brancaster. There must be a copy of Brancaster's book in his library. If there was, Foxe hoped it could throw some light on the mystery. Some of the groups associated with cults could be vindictive if their secrets were compromised. Richard Logan was said always to be greedy for money. Could he have tried to sell some of his father's carvings? It was a possibility.

He left the thought for later. Now he must make plans for dealing with the ringers.

What he needed to know was whether any of them spent enough time alone with Mr Logan after the practice session to bring about his death. The rest of the evening was of no importance. Of course, he had to assume the actual murderer, if he was one of their number, would lie about his movements. The most he could achieve would be to discover who *might* have spent time with Logan after the rest had left. The more he thought about it, the more he felt sure his purpose should be to establish who had left alone. Any of them could have turned back in secret after the others had gone. Mr Tate had said Mr Logan always stayed behind to clear up and leave all safe. That must make those who left alone, or split from their companions soon after leaving, his principal suspects. Those who left in a group or in pairs, then stayed together as they walked home, could be dismissed.

That would do for this evening. What else after that?

He should return to Logan's house and talk again with the house-keeper, Mrs Baker. He and the alderman had only exchanged a few words with her, yet she must see what went on in that house. She might well also know something of Logan's family history. Servants always understood more about their masters' business than those upstairs estimated. Would she be prepared to speak freely? To question her again must be high on his list.

What of the man Charlie's little guttersnipes said was still hanging around the house? Where did he fit in? If he was a sailor or a fisherman, Yarmouth or Lowestoft would be the places to look for traces of him. He mustn't forget King's Lynn either. There was plenty of coastal shipping there, as well as whalers and the Baltic timber trade. Of course, the fellow might have nothing to do with Logan's death. Everyone in Norwich assumed Richard Logan kept ample wealth hidden in his house. All misers did in popular imagination. Now Logan was dead without an heir, so the man could simply be trying to take advantage of a house he thought would be empty.

Foxe knew it would take days to talk to all these people. That would be more than enough for the burglar to succeed in breaking in or decide to give up and leave. He must move much quicker. It was risky, but it was the only way he could see to make progress. If possible, he would take the man by surprise and force the truth out of him.

🔆 10 🔆

THE MAN OF ACTION

oxe never took his breakfast before nine o'clock. The day after
his visit to Mr Logan's house and the bell-ringing proved
different. First, he managed to upset Molly by rising at seven
and demanding hot water for washing and shaving. She had only just
set a kettle to boil, so he had to wait, which made both of them irrita-
ble. Mrs Whitbread, his cook, was the next to be thrown into confusion. He entered his parlour soon after eight and demanded coffee and
fresh rolls immediately. Neither were ready. By this time, Alfred, the
valet, was on the alert and he laid out Foxe's morning gown ready for
him. It was promptly rejected. Instead, the flustered man was told to
bring outdoor clothes. Once dressed, Foxe finally went out, leaving his
household in a state of angry turmoil, like an ant's nest poked with a
stick.

Where he was going and for what purpose became the sole topic of
conversation amongst the servants. None could come up with an
answer to either question. By this time, Mrs Crombie and Miss
Benfield had arrived. Charlie, fresh from joining in the frantic speculation in the kitchen, hurried into the shop to acquaint them with his
master's unexpected break with his usual habits.

Foxe was absent for about an hour. When he returned, he

produced even more chaos. He summoned Charlie and sent him with an urgent message to Alderman Halloran. That done, he was to seek out the grocer, George Tate, and ask him where three of the bell-ringers lived. The ones he was interested in were Messrs Gradnor, Ovenden and Rogerstone. Last, the lad was to find the street children and organise for three or four of them to go with Foxe on a mission the next night. The rest were to resume their watch on the burglar and be sure to keep Charlie informed of his movements.

Foxe called Molly and told her to inform Mrs Whitbread that he would take his dinner at four as usual. Supper was to be at ten. Florence he sent into the shop with a note for Mrs Crombie, warning her that Charlie would be absent most of the day on the errands Foxe had given him. In it, Foxe also asked her to spread a rumour that Logan's servants would be leaving his house for a few days, beginning on the morrow. The story would be that Mrs Baker had asked leave to visit a sick relative in Beccles and Jane would go with her. It was essential that as many people as possible should get this news, so Miss Benfield should join in. Miss Gravener too, if she was willing.

Of his own movements, Foxe said nothing. He left his home again, saying he would return sometime after noon.

His destination was Logan's house. He didn't know anything of the housekeeper's daily habits, so he could only hope she was in when he arrived. His luck held and she answered the door to his knock. It was almost as if she had been expecting him to come. She asked no questions about his visit, took him into the dining room and brought him coffee. Then she sat on a chair opposite and waited for him to state his business. All this time, she had showed no signs of nervousness or of surprise.

By the time Foxe left, some two hours later, his thoughts about Logan's death were much more focused. He had the details of the burglar's visit on the night of Logan's death. He knew there had been another intruder, the following night, who had entered through the front door, presumably by using a key taken from Logan's body. Taken together, this suggested the burglar and the murderer were different people.

He had begun by talking to Mrs Baker about the burglar.

"He managed to get through the scullery window," Mrs Baker told him. "I usually left it open for the cat. Jane heard the noise and went to investigate. She came to wake me on her way."

"Jane?"

"Jane Thaxter, the other servant. She's much younger than I am, sir, and quite a strapping, vigorous woman. We surprised the intruder together and he ran back to the scullery at once. Before we could grab his legs, he'd slithered through the window and was making off up the garden. Nothing seemed to be missing. We assumed he'd been thwarted by all the locked doors."

"Quite likely. Do you know if he tried again?"

"We're not sure. The next night someone else got in, but this time he came through the front door. Whether this was the same man or another I don't know, sir. Jane heard the noise and went to investigate. Whoever it was ran off as soon as he caught sight of her."

"She sounds to be a brave young woman, Mrs Baker."

"She is, sir, no doubt about it. That time she hadn't even stopped to wake me. I only discovered what had happened after the man had gone."

"Can you recall exactly what Jane said? I'm eager to identify both these intruders, if I can. Even a casual remark might be useful in tracking down who they were. The first one, the one who came through the window, I may have already found. The second one puzzles me. It can't have been the same person. If he had a key, why come through the window the first night? The man I have my eye on has been back most nights since then and appears to be searching for a way in. That doesn't suggest he ever had a key. Please give me Jane's exact words, if you can."

"I should explain about Jane, sir. The poor girl is dumb. Maybe it's because of this that her hearing is so much sharper than most people's. When she first came, she could only make inarticulate noises. I've taught her to write well enough to scribble words on a writing slate and she always carries it around with her. It's a slow way to express herself, sir, so you rarely get any detail. I don't think she saw much anyway."

"Why is that?"

"When she woke me, she wrote that she'd heard noises, gone to the hall and surprised someone about to go up the stairs. At the first sight of her, he — that's what she wrote — had given a scream of terror and rushed out of the front door, leaving it open. Maybe he thought Jane was a ghost, sir. She was wearing a white nightdress and she wouldn't have stopped to light a candle. We both know our way around quite well in the dark."

Mrs Baker had also proved to be a mine of information on her late employer's daily habits. He spent most of his time in the study where his desk was. She knew he went there to write letters, cast the accounts and send out bills. Much of the rest of the time he spent writing out long columns of figures. She didn't know exactly what these were, but assumed they were to do with change-ringing, since that was his main passion. Sometimes he wrote in a large book. She thought he was working something out by means of the columns of numbers, then writing down the results.

He rarely went to the workshop. In the early days after his father's death, he'd shown more interest in the business, but that had declined. Nowadays, he rarely even dealt with customers who came to order a coffin and hire a bier for a funeral. If he was at home and not busy with anything else, he might see one or two in a month, but no more. She thought the workmen also made things like door and window frames, standard items, but she wasn't sure. All the special work they had taken on when his father was alive ceased on his death.

How long ago had that been? More than ten years, she said. He hadn't been well for some while. Mr James had always been an active man, travelling all over the county to visit customers, draw up plans and supervise work. At first, he only had to stay at home for short periods. Then these grew longer, until he was confined to the house. In some ways, his death had been a blessing.

Foxe asked whether all the carvings in the library were James Logan's work.

"Oh yes, sir. Towards the end, when he couldn't go out, he took great comfort in still being able to do what he loved most, which was to carve in wood. He missed the conversations he had enjoyed with the Earl of Brancaster a great deal though. I believe they talked about ancient things, stories of the past and the beliefs of the people who lived back then. My master told me that the pictures he carved on the library panels were based on legends and beliefs the earl had written down in his book. It amused him to try to turn the earl's words into scenes."

"There's a large bronze —"

"Not bronze, sir. Wood. Some type of special wood from foreign parts. Very hard and dense, the master said it was. Ideal for tiny details, but tricky to carve. He was proud of that carving. Very proud."

"I hope you won't think me indelicate, Mrs Baker, but I did notice it's ... err ... quite explicit."

She laughed.

"He told me that because he'd carved it for himself, it didn't matter if he ignored some of the conventions, sir. He wouldn't have done that if he'd intended to sell it or was doing it for a commission."

"I expect not."

"No one goes into the library now, so the statue does no harm. If the contents of the house have to be sold, I imagine it'll be altered or burned. It's a shame to ruin such a fine carving, but there it is. The one who made it is dead, as is his son. It won't matter to either what becomes of it."

"No other children?"

"A daughter, but she eloped years ago and hasn't been heard of since. She never got in touch, even when her father died. We couldn't write to her since we didn't know where she was. News of his death was in the newspapers though, so it ought to have reached her, if she was still alive herself."

Later, they talked of other matters, but dealing with those would have to wait a little. First there was a burglar to be caught.

Foxe returned to his house shortly before one and found Charlie waiting for him. He'd done all his master asked, he said. Five of the street children would be ready the next night for whatever Mr Foxe wanted them to do. He had obtained the addresses for the three bell-ringers from a puzzled Mr Tate. Mrs Crombie had written them down to make sure they were correct. Charlie's writing was still wayward and his spelling more imaginative than precise. He'd also brought back a message from Alderman Halloran saying the constables would be ready as Mr Foxe had asked. He had also brought an invitation for his master to dine with the Halloran family the day after tomorrow, if that was convenient. The alderman was eager to hear the latest news.

Foxe told Charlie to wait to take his message of acceptance back to the alderman. After that, he could return to his work. He wrote letters to Mr Rogerstone and Mr Ovenden and sent Alfred to deliver them. He should ask Mrs Crombie for their addresses. In the letters, Foxe asked to call on each man the next day, either at home or at his place of work, as he chose. He had decided to deal with Mr Gradnor in another way. That depended on the alderman being willing to fall in with his plans. He had never involved Halloran in one of his investigations before. This time, Foxe could see no way of reaching a successful conclusion by any other means.

WITH TIME TO OCCUPY BEFORE DINNER, FOXE DECIDED TO SEE IF Mrs Crombie was free to talk. He wanted to be quite sure of the various actions he needed to undertake. Since Brock was away, she was the only person he could talk things over with.

The moment he entered the shop, Charlie rushed up and drew Foxe aside into the stockroom.

"I forgot, Master. I forget to tell you."

"What did you forget?"

"My friends have found where that man is staying. They followed him back last night, as you said, instead of staying to watch the house. At least, some stayed and some followed. That way they made sure they missed nothing."

"That was very sensible of them, Charlie. So some followed this man —"

"He went to a lower-class lodging house across the water in Fishgate Street. Some of them know it well enough. It's the sort of place the wherrymen use and sometimes a sailor who's decided Norwich is a better place to spend his pay than Yarmouth. The owner is a one-eyed drunk who used to work on the river. His wife helps him. She's a real slut and dirty with it."

"Hmm. Our mystery man doesn't have much money to spare, it seems. Did they say what he's been doing this morning?"

"Wandering about, as if he's trying to pass the time. They were still with him when I caught up with them, so they pointed him out. He was sitting on a pile of empty boxes on the old wharf by Fye Bridge, smoking and staring at the river."

"Waiting for dark. We'll see whether he goes back to Logan's house tonight. If he does, he won't get inside. I've warned the housekeeper to make sure to shutter and bar all the windows and lock the doors."

"What's he doing, Master?"

"Getting more and more frustrated. There's something— or he thinks there is — inside that house. Whatever it is, he wants it very badly. Otherwise he would have given up by now and gone to rob somewhere easier. By the way, do your friends think he knows the city?"

"Not at all. They say he sticks to one or two areas, as if he's not used to such a big town and is afraid he might get lost."

"That's most interesting. I'll think about it. Anything else to tell me?"

"No, Master. That's all."

"Very well, lad. Go into the shop and see if Mrs Crombie is serving anyone. If not, ask her to come through into my parlour to hear the latest news about the murder. You had best come as well."

They arrived hot on Mr Foxe's heels and sat down, eager to hear whatever he was going to tell them. Charlie was not usually allowed in the room, save to bring messages, so this was a treat.

"There are several matters I need to explain," Foxe said, "but first I need to tell you what I learned yesterday. As you know, I went to St. Peter Mancroft to meet the group of bell-ringers. When I got there, Mr Tate was fussing around with arrangements for what he called a 'touch' to be rung 'muffled' next Sunday in Logan's memory."

"Do you have any idea what that means?" Mrs Crombie said.

"I asked them. A touch means a short sequence of changes, perhaps lasting up to an hour. They muffle the bells by strapping leather pads to the clappers to make the bells sound quiet and dull. Sad rather than

THIS PARODY OF DEATH

joyful. Apparently doing this for someone who's died is a high honour amongst the bell-ringing fraternity."

"Did they tell you anything useful when you got to speak with them?"

"As I expected, they were all determined not to speak ill of the dead. All I got in response to direct questions about Mr Logan was praise of his ability and dedication as a ringer.

"He was well liked then?"

"Well-respected certainly. I'm not sure how much people liked him. No one amongst the group was going to breathe a word of criticism yesterday. I just got the feeling there were a good many tensions they were hiding from me. Of course, it might be no more than the fact they had nothing to do. They had agreed at the start of the evening the bells would stay silent out of respect for the dead."

"So it was a waste of your time going, Master."

"No, Charlie, I wouldn't say that. I met all but one of those who were present the night Logan was murdered. Last evening nine ringers were present. The week before, there were eleven — including Logan of course.

"So who was missing?"

"A man called Mr Gradnor. I gather he's a kind of attorney or factor. Someone who acts in local matters for merchants and manufacturers from London or overseas. He collects payment for them, pays bills and then sends them the balance. Every so often, he makes a complete accounting for the sums involved. He's highly trusted and handles hundreds of pounds every week. They pay him by letting him deduct an agreed percentage from the amount he sends on to them. He also 'holds the purse' — acts as the treasurer — for the bell-ringers."

"Why do they need a treasurer?" Mrs Crombie asked.

"All the ringers contribute small amounts of money each week. Some goes towards the cost of feasts at Christmas and Easter. The group also acts as a kind of friendly society. The treasurer pays out cash to help members in times of sickness or financial stress. There have also been large bequests of money or land to meet the costs of keeping the bells in good order. From time to time, for example, they need various items like new bell ropes. When they can, they raise money for specific improvements. Mr Tate told me the treble bell needs replacing. It's the oldest bell in the tower and several hundred years of the clash of clapper against rim has worn the metal away. Now it's starting to sound flat. Soon it will crack and become useless. They want to have it melted down and recast with fresh bronze to bring it back to the right weight."

"Did you learn why Mr Gradnor was absent?"

"No one knew. It seems they live all around the city and walk to and from the tower alone or in small groups. In fact, that was the most useful information I got. Leaving aside Logan, the other ten ringers left the week before in more or less the usual order. Five of them live in the direction of the river, in the streets of Mid-Wymer ward. They come and go together and did so on that evening. Tate's shop is the other side of the Hay Market. It's not far for him and he comes and goes alone. The other four are scattered in the streets between the Chapel Field and Pottergate Street. Two of them sometimes walk home together, though they more often come and go on their own. That's what they said they did the night of Mr Logan's murder. One of those two is Mr Gradnor. The other is Mr Ovenden. He said he went to The White Swan for a beer before going home."

"And the other two?" Mrs Crombie had been counting.

"That's a man called Mr Rogerstone and another by name of Barnham. Mr Rogerstone is a weaver, like Mr Ovenden. He lives near Charing Cross. He said he left with Mr Barnham. They may have left together but they soon parted. Mr Rogerstone noticed he'd lost his stick and wanted to look for it. Mr Barnham said he needed to get home and went on alone. "

"Sounds as if everyone is accounted for," Mrs Crombie said.

"Or lying," Charlie added. Mrs Crombie looked at him sharply.

"Quite right, Charlie," Foxe said. "A mixture, I suspect. I don't think Mr Tate is involved. He's much too nervous. I can't see him taking desperate measures against anyone. It's possible, but for the moment I'm going to rule him out. Now Logan's dead, he's acting as Tower Captain until an election can be held. I think he'll be delighted to give it up. He may not even let his own name go forward. A natural lieutenant, our Mr Tate, not a captain."

"That leaves three: Mr Gradnor, Mr Rogerstone and Mr Ovenden. Mr Barnham too, I suppose."

"I doubt it's him. He's quite new to the team and lives the furthest away. He said he hurried and caught up with the other five by the castle. They confirm that, so unless they're lying he couldn't have had time to return to the tower. I definitely can't rule out any of the other three, especially Mr Gradnor. His absence last night may be nothing, but it's strange. I also think there's something odd between Mr Rogerstone and Mr Ovenden, the two weavers. When Mr Rogerstone said he went straight home, Mr Ovenden gave him quite a sharp look. Did he know it wasn't true?"

"Mr Ovenden's own tale of going to The White Swan for a tankard of ale strikes me as weak," Mrs Crombie said. "It would be hard to disprove though. Any friends who were there could be persuaded to confirm his story."

"Indeed so. Mr Ovenden said he must have been leaving The White Swan about twenty minutes after the practice ended. When he did so, I could have sworn Mr Rogerstone looked frightened. Remember he claimed to have left with Mr Barnham, who's a fishmonger, and walked along with him. But Mr Barnham, though he agreed he'd left with Rogerstone, said he walked most of his way home alone. That statement was backed up by five of the others who walked part of the way with him."

"I'm getting confused," Mrs Crombie said.

"So was I," Foxe agreed, "so I wrote it all down and worked out the sequence. Eight of the ringers came down from the tower in a body. Five of them left and walked home together. Mr Barnham caught them up and walked with them some of the way. We can ignore all of them, unless they're covering up for one of their number. I doubt that. The other three men we've been talking about left at the same time as the rest. Two say they went straight home. One says he went to get a drink and went home a little later. That left Mr Tate and Mr Logan. Mr Tate said he usually helped with the clearing up, then left with Mr Logan. However, that night he was in a hurry because his wife had been feeling unwell during the afternoon. He was worried about her, but she had insisted he went to the practice as usual. Mr Logan said he would see to the clearing up and Mr Tate should go home to his wife. Mr Tate went home less than five minutes after the others, leaving Mr Logan alone in the tower."

"Thank you, Mr Foxe. That's clearer now. So how are you going to proceed?"

"I've sent messages to the three men we've been talking about, asking to speak to them as soon as possible. Perhaps they'll tell me more on their own."

❧ II ❧

MANY A SLIP

F oxe woke next morning so full of vitality and excitement he
surprised himself. Events were moving at last. He had a sense
of purpose and a plan of action to follow. It was going to be an
excellent day. He was so eager to get started that he jumped out of bed
and began striding up and down the room. He even attempted to sing.
This was such a disturbing noise that Molly left the hot water for his
morning wash and shave on the landing outside and fled back to the
kitchen. It was left to Alfred to tap warily on Foxe's door and bring the
jug of hot water inside. He sidled in, leaving the door open in case he
needed to make a dash for safety.

Washed, shaved and dressed in his morning gown, Foxe hurried
down the stairs for his morning coffee and rolls. Molly was still uncertain about the safety of approaching her master on her own, so she
carried the coffee pot in, while Florence, the kitchen maid, followed
with a plate of hot rolls wrapped in a clean cloth. They put these down
and slipped out as quickly as they could. Foxe meanwhile was staring
out of the window, watching a thrush smashing a snail against a stone.

Foxe was always a hearty eater at breakfast. This morning he
surpassed himself. He consumed all the rolls in record time, then
called for Molly to bring him more —butter and jam as well. As a

result, he was a good deal less energetic by the time Charlie plucked up the courage to enter. Foxe looked at his apprentice with what he considered to be a kindly eye. To the boy, it looked more like rampant dyspepsia, accompanied as it was by a series of burps and hiccups.

"Morning, Master." Charlie chose a neutral opening.

"Morning, my boy. A beautiful morning it is too. The sun is shining and the sky is blue. Spring seems to be here at last. I was watching a thrush smashing a snail's shell against a stone. Quite fascinating. Have you ever seen thrushes do that?"

Charlie admitted he had not. He could have added that he wouldn't be able to tell a thrush from an eagle. However, he judged his master's mood too uncertain for anything that might be interpreted as answering back.

"You should, you know," Foxe said, burping again. "Part of your education. Get Mrs Crombie to take you for a long walk in one of the pleasure grounds and show you where to look. Good heavens! I seem to be plagued with hiccups this morning. Too much yeast in the rolls, I expect. Do you get hiccups?"

By now Charlie was convinced his master was either drunk or showing the first signs of madness. He decided to give him his message and leave right away.

"Got a message from Janie, Master. She says everything is ready for tonight."

"Excellent, excellent. Ask Molly to bring me more coffee, lad. I need to sit here a while longer before I go out. Let my breakfast go down a little."

Mr Foxe was well behind his usual schedule by the time he called for Alfred to bring his waistcoat and jacket so he could walk to the coffeehouse. Not that it mattered much. He couldn't proceed with the investigation until he heard from Mr Ovenden and Mr Rogerstone.

Disappointment awaited him on his return. Both men had replied that they wouldn't be available that day. Mr Rogerstone said the earliest he could manage would be the following afternoon. Mr Ovenden asked for an even longer delay.

That was the problem with weavers. Most were outworkers, who kept their looms in their own houses and relied on orders from a single master weaver. None received regular wages. They were paid according to the finished goods they delivered. Since they could only work in daylight, they were busy at their looms from dawn to dusk. Any interruption to this meant less finished cloth and a consequent loss of earnings.

Mr Rogerstone wrote that he needed to see the master weaver. The workman who brought his orders and arranged for fresh supplies of yarn had failed to turn up at the appointed time. He had woven cloth ready to collect, but no fresh orders to begin on or yarn to weave with. If he did no work, he received no pay. He had four children to feed, so could not afford to be idle. Mr Ovenden's excuse was similar. He was working on a large order, he wrote, which he had to finish in a set time. He couldn't afford to finish late. He was behind already and the master weaver was threatening to stop using him.

Foxe now had nothing to occupy his time before the constables came at nine in the evening. It was vital to enter Mr Logan's house with as little fuss as possible, so he'd decided to go with the constables. If he didn't, they would forget his instructions and arrive with a great stamping of boots. Parish constables were more noted for brawn and aggression than brains. It would be foolish to rely on them any more than was essential.

It wasn't likely the burglar would arrive much before eleven. Still, Foxe wanted them all inside and concealed in good time. This might well be their only chance to take him. If they had to return a second or third time, the chance of scaring the man off would rise a great deal.

Foxe was standing in the hall, wondering how to fill his time, when Charlie came in from outside. Seeing his master standing there, he couldn't contain his excitement.

"Master! Master! I got important news for you. I was going to ask Molly to see if I could disturb you, but now you're here —"

"What is it, boy? Come into the parlour, take a seat and then tell me what's brought you here. I can see you're excited. Calm down and tell me in the proper order."

Foxe hoped some of the street children might have seen the ringers leaving St. Peter Mancroft on the night of Logan's death. Charlie had spread the word around to that effect. Now a group of children had come with their response. This was exactly the tonic Foxe needed. He'd come away from his meeting with the ringers sure he'd been given only lies and half-truths. Now he hoped to hear the truth. Here he was, trusting a group of street children more than respectable men. It was a strange world.

"Where are they?"

"In the garden, Master, waiting to speak to you."

"I'll go at once. You go back to Mrs Crombie. If I take you from your duties even more, she'll be angry with me. Don't worry. I'll let you know what they tell me."

"I know, Master. They told me first."

WHAT THESE CHILDREN TOLD FOXE WAS SO IMPORTANT HE determined to note it down before he forgot any of the details. He therefore retired to his library immediately after dinner, taking a candle holder with him and a supply of good wax candles. The more Foxe thought about it, the surer he'd become that the ringers hadn't all gone straight home as they claimed. The children's story confirmed this.

He took up his quill, dipped it into the ink and began to write. The first sheet of paper he headed "Bell-ringers". Below that heading, he wrote the names of his suspects in the ringing team. He labelled a second sheet "Logan Household". There he wrote the names of Richard Logan, Mrs Baker and Jane Thaxter. He wondered whether to write Hester Logan as well, but concluded that should wait. After hesitating a moment, he set the second sheet aside. Begin at the beginning. No distractions.

The children had told him they nearly always slept in the churchyard at St Peter Mancroft. The best place was an angle of the church wall between the aisle and the tower. Being enclosed on two sides, they were protected from winds from the east and the south. A large table tomb blocked winds from the north. Westerlies they had to endure. Rain had been a problem until a kindly parishioner gave them a pair of old blankets. They spread these on the ground and made a kind of tent amongst the tombstones. For a roof they had a piece of thick tarpaulin, green with age but still waterproof. Under there, five or six of them would huddle together in tolerable comfort on all but the coldest nights.

This time of year, the end of the ringing practice was their signal to bed down. Before then it was too noisy. Most sat and talked, while a few of the older ones kept watch for unwary passers-by whose pockets could be picked. Once the bell-ringers were heard leaving, everyone settled down in their hideout and tried to sleep.

They remembered that evening, they said, because they kept being disturbed. It started as normal with the ringers saying their good-nights, then splitting up and walking away in groups. Shortly after-wards, another man came out of the church on his own. He set off across the Market Place. That was also typical. What happened next was not.

The children had little sense of the passing of time. That made it hard to get a clear idea how long after the bulk of the ringers had gone home things started to happen. "Later" or "a bit later" was the best they could offer. They hadn't settled themselves down, they said, so it couldn't have been very long. Two men came to the tower and both went inside. They hadn't come together. One had followed the other, though the gap between them wasn't great. No, they hadn't looked furtive. More determined. They must have met inside for certain, because they came out together. Were they inside for a long time? No, they came out quite quickly. What did these men do then? They talked together for a bit. Could anyone hear what they said? No, but they sounded angry. After a short while, they walked off in different directions.

Foxe noted this down in summary form. The two men he decided to call 'A' and 'B'. They had gone inside, presumably to speak with Richard Logan. Whatever their business, it hadn't taken long to state it and get a response. Since the children said their discussion before they parted was angry, they must have been turned down.

After 'A' and 'B' had gone, there was another gap. How long? About the same as the first, the children thought. Another man came through the churchyard. He did look furtive, they said. It was clear he didn't want to be seen. He kept stopping as if he was listening. They also thought he wasn't sure of his way. It took him several moments to find the tower door and go inside. Foxe labelled this man 'C'.

'C' had only just gone inside when someone else came. This time it was a woman. Young or old? They couldn't tell. She was all muffled up. Tall or short? This caused some argument. To the smaller children, all adults looked tall. They thought she was "a lanky kind of woman." Others said she wasn't short, but not particularly tall either. Could they see the colour of her hair or anything about her face? It was quite dark by then. She did have a lantern, but kept it low to see where she was putting her feet. Anyway, she had a shawl over her head, so her face was almost hidden. Nice clothes? Ordinary, they said. Like a labourer's wife or a servant.

Could they tell him anything else about her? She knew where she was going, they agreed. She went to the door and slipped inside right away. This amused them. Since the man was still there, they assumed she was joining him by arrangement. That meant she had to be either a whore or a woman up to no good. She and the man obviously hoped to conduct their business in comfort inside the church. Perhaps one of the ringers had left the door open for them. If that wasn't the explanation, the two would be in for a surprise. If anyone was still inside, he'd lock up behind him, shutting them in until morning. The children thought this was a fine joke. Imagine everyone's faces when the verger arrived to open the church next day!

The flickering of his candles was making it hard for Foxe to see what he was writing. He got up to close and bar the shutters against draughts. That made it better, though writing by candlelight was never easy.

He sat down at his desk again and returned to his task. This was the only woman the children had seen, so he labelled her 'W'. Four people so far. 'A' and 'B' follow one another inside and leave together. 'C' arrives on his own, but is then joined by 'W', maybe for sex, maybe not. He doesn't know where he's going, but she does.

It hadn't ended there. The children were surprised to see the man leave within a minute or two of the woman arriving. One of the older boys suggested he could hardly have got his money's worth. A girl who earned her food the same way sneered at him. She said many men couldn't last long enough for you to get comfortable. It was as well she did it for money. If she wanted pleasure, she'd be disappointed far too often. This caused such mirth they almost missed the last arrival. This was another man. Foxe, still writing his notes, called him 'D'. 'C' had left, but 'W' was still there.

By then, the children were convinced a whore had arranged for the tower door to be left open so she could entertain her customers in the church. Who might have done this, they couldn't imagine. Some said it must be one of the ringers. The rest thought the verger was the one who had set up the racket. He might be an ugly old man, but he liked money as much as anyone.

They were still arguing the point when they saw the man leave. Another 'quickie'. The woman came out a few moments later, pulled the door shut behind her, but didn't lock it. Either she had no key or she intended to return for a second lot of men. They didn't think that happened, but they went to sleep after she left. If she had come back, they missed her. That was it. Five people. 'A' and 'B' arrive together — or almost — 'C' and 'D' spend time separately with the woman, 'W'. What on earth could it mean? Foxe sat back to think about it when he heard his clock strike the half hour. If that was half-past eight, he needed to leave things there and get ready to catch a burglar. He tidied his papers into a draw, put away the pen, closed the inkwell and blew out all but one of the candles in the holder. One would be enough to see by to go up to his room and get ready.

12

TAKEN BY SURPRISE

Charlie shifted on the chair yet again. The hard seat must be affecting him the same way mine is hurting me, Foxe thought. My backside has better padding than his too. He's not used to sitting still doing nothing. Lord, my feet are cold.

Foxe bent over to whisper in Charlie's ear — or where he presumed his ear to be. It was so dark in the hallway of Logan's house he could see nothing at all. It didn't matter whether his eyes were open or closed. Nothing. The place had better shutters than his own house. Even with those closed, there were always a few gleams of light that got through.

"Try to stay still, if you can. You'd be surprised how loud someone fidgeting can sound."

"I am trying, but my bottom hurts. Do you know what time it is, Master?"

"I heard eleven strike a little while ago. Remind me again when he's been coming."

"Janie said he usually comes between now and midnight. I expect he doesn't want to risk the old witch at the lodging house where he's staying locking him out."

Foxe muttered something about keeping quiet to listen better. In fact, he could hear too much, not too little. Odd, how a long period when you couldn't see, sharpened your other senses. Now he could hear every one of the creakings and groanings all houses made during the night. One or two faint sounds even penetrated from the street. Several times he thought he detected the swift pattering of mice. Once it was followed by a soft thud and a shrill squeak. Mrs Baker's cat must be somewhere about, doing the job she kept it for.

The keenness of his sense of smell had also increased. There was a strong scent of furniture polish. Mrs Baker and Jane had been busy. He wondered what else they found to do, all alone in this house.

He could also distinguish another faint odour. What was it? Bread. That was it. The housekeeper or Jane had been baking. His stomach growled. He'd eaten supper before coming out, but that smell of freshly made bread, feeble as it was, was making him hungry.

"Was that your stomach, Master?"

"I'm afraid so, lad. It's the smell of bread."

"Bread? I thought it was pastry."

They had arrived soon after nine. Not through the street at the front, of course. Too visible. Mrs Baker let them in through the gate in the rear wall, then the back door, locking it behind them. Nothing must alarm their visitor to make him suspect a trap. The only change from past nights was that Jane had left the scullery window ajar, as if for the cat. That's how it had been the first time he came. Foxe hoped he wouldn't see it as unusual.

The two constables Alderman Halloran had loaned them were in the kitchen. Foxe could only hope they were staying alert. It wasn't likely the burglar would go in there. Not if he remembered the layout of the house from his previous visit. Even so, Foxe made the two of them erect a screen of clothes to hide behind. It would look as if the garments had been put there to dry overnight.

He decided to stay in the hallway. Charlie, of course, stuck close to him. At first, they thought they'd have to conceal themselves in the parlour. The burglar would need to bring a candle or a lantern if he wanted to see his way. Either would be bright enough to reveal anyone in the open. It was Mrs Baker who pointed out the screen used to conceal the way to the servants' quarter and back stairs. By shifting it to one side, they could sit behind it, which was what they were doing now. It meant they would be close to where the burglar must pass, if he came from the scullery as before.

What was that? Foxe stiffened, then relaxed as a warm, furry body pressed against his leg. Cats could see in the dark, so this one must be wondering what the two humans were doing. He bent forward and stroked it once or twice, then it wandered away.

Foxe pondered where in the house the children had hidden themselves. He'd reasoned they would know more about staying out of sight than he did, so let them choose for themselves. He'd given them only two instructions. Make sure the man doesn't escape, whatever else happens, and don't steal anything. He'd asked Mrs Baker to leave some cutlery and plates on the dining table. There were also one or two nice ornaments on mantels and side tables. If the burglar took any, they would have grounds to hold him in prison until they could understand his true purpose.

Another noise. A kind of scuffling, too heavy to be the cat this time. It came from behind them, in the direction of the kitchen. Then a sound both could recognise, the striking of flint on steel. Someone was kindling a flame to light a candle.

Foxe's heart was beating so much he feared the burglar must hear it. At last he could see a faint light. The man had ignored the servant's area, as they hoped. He was coming towards the hall. Where now? The stealthy footsteps came much too close before moving off again. He must be going into the dining room. Foxe could hear furtive movements, then the chink of metal.

He decided to risk bending to look around the edge of the screen. Now he could see the light from a candle moving about by the table, then going further away. More clattering. It seemed the burglar had decided he didn't need to be so cautious. He was coming back towards the front door, Foxe leaned back, careful to stay out of sight.

By watching how the candlelight moved on the ceiling, Foxe worked out the man had walked past them and gone into the parlour. He could hear drawers opening and once the click of a key turned in a lock. Their false tale that the house was empty must have reached him. He would never have been so careless if he thought there would be people asleep somewhere. The flickering light had stopped moving. The man must be working out where to go next.

Foxe decided they had waited long enough. He didn't want the man to go upstairs. The front door was locked and bolted, as was the back entry. The only means of escape would be to go back the way he had come. That meant passing the kitchen where the constables were. Pray God they were still awake and alert.

As the man came closer, heading towards the door to the stairs, Foxe decided to strike. He stood up, took a step to the side and yelled "Stop thief!". He saw the burglar start, recover with astonishing speed and dash for the way back to the scullery. His candle blew out as he ran and Foxe could see no more. He only heard some muffled scampering followed by a loud crash. Then an even louder yell of anger and fear.

Fortunately, the constables were awake. They must have heard the man come in and lit their lanterns from the kitchen range. Now they rushed through from the rear of the house, lanterns held high and truncheons at the ready. A few moments later, Mrs Baker and Jane came from their bedrooms where Foxe had told them to wait. Each carried a candleholder with four large candles ready lit.

The light revealed an unexpected scene. The burglar was face down on the floor, writhing under the weight of three of the four boys and the two girls sitting on his back and legs. The other boy had hold of the thief's head and was banging it rhythmically on the wood of the floor. The constables needed to rescue him, not wrestle him into submission. They pushed the children aside, shackled the man's hands behind him and dragged him to his feet.

A younger man than Foxe had expected, barely more than twenty years old. Dirty from the floor, but otherwise tolerably well dressed. Dark clothes, shabby but clean. As the children had reported, he looked like a sailor, with a tanned and weather-beaten face and a short beard.

Charlie came to stand by Foxe. "Here's 'is bag," one of the girls said. "The measly cove 'ad it in 'is 'and when 'e tripped over me. I crouched down on purpose see, so he'd fall over."

"Well done," Foxe said quietly. "I hope he didn't hurt you."

"Nah! In such an 'urry, 'e pitched right over me and fell on 'is head."

"See what's in the bag," Foxe told one of the constables.

"Spoons, a salt cellar, two candlesticks, several china ornaments —"

"Bloody 'ell!" his colleague said. "Thass more'n enough to stretch 'is neck twice over."

Foxe should have been feeling triumphant. He'd got his man. No one was hurt. Instead he felt disappointed, even despondent. It looked as if this was a common burglar. Foxe had been positive that wasn't the case. Ah well, so he'd been wrong again.

"Well, fellow?" he said. "Do you have anything to say for yourself?"

The man seemed too angry to speak. Instead, he tried to spit at Foxe. One of the constables realised what he was intending and punched him in the stomach, hard enough to double him over.

"Insolence is never a good idea," Foxe said. "It'll only make things worse for you."

He turned to the constables.

"Take him away and make sure you don't lose him. A night in the lock-up might amend his manners. Tell the turnkey to bring him before Alderman Halloran. I expect he'll convene a sitting of the magistrates sometime tomorrow. You can give evidence of how and where we found him and what he was carrying."

The constables dragged the man towards the front door, then waited while Mrs Baker unlocked it and drew back the bolts. Foxe turned away to hand out pennies and praise in equal measure. Some of the children slipped out after the constables. Foxe had told them to make sure the man didn't escape. He believed in being doubly sure.

"A common burglar," Foxe said, half to himself. "I was so certain ..."

Mrs Baker stepped over. "I've seen him before," she said. "It's the man who came the day the master was killed and asked to talk to him. That's right, isn't it Jane?"

The young maid nodded vigorously.

"She mightn't be able to speak, Mr Foxe, but there's nothing wrong with her eyes. What's going to happen to him?"

"The magistrates will commit him to the assize or the next Quarter Sessions for trial. He'll be found guilty, since we caught him in the act. By stealing that amount, he may well have sentenced himself to death. It's still possible he may not hang, I suppose. It all depends on how he comes over to the judge and whether he's known for any previous crimes. If he shows penitence and hasn't much of a record, he'll be transported to the colonies in America. You know, Mrs Baker. I felt so sure there was something behind his visits other than theft. It bothers me to have been proved so wrong."

"If you talk with him, sir, ask him if he's been to Norwich before. Perhaps he was born here, or lived here for a time. There's something familiar about his face, but I can't put my finger on it. Now, sir. Jane made some bread and pastries this afternoon. She's a wonder at baking, the master always used to say so. I wonder if you and your apprentice —"

They didn't wait to hear more.

13

A TIME OF MADNESS

Foxe woke the next morning with the disappointment fresh in his mind. He wondered why he had ever thought there was more to the man they had taken last night than theft. Even his persistence in revisiting the house night after night could be explained. He must have credited the popular belief Logan was a miser with a hidden hoard of treasure. Foxe had wanted a different story and a different reason for the crime. He'd hoped it wouldn't turn out to be as pointless and predictable as usual.

He shifted slightly against the pillows, trying to counter the stiffness brought on by last night's long wait on a hard chair. The window shutters were closed and the bed curtains pulled across. Too dark to see the clock. The house was quiet. Just a few sounds, far off, suggesting activity starting up in the kitchen. Early then. A good time to reflect.

He'd never been able to convince himself Logan's death was due to a random attack or some dispute amongst the bell-ringers. People could become obsessive about some activity. He knew that. But wouldn't the urge to kill come from something far more basic to human nature? He'd known hatred, jealousy, greed and anger drive a person to commit murder, never a pastime like ringing changes. Yet

THIS PARODY OF DEATH

he'd been told change-ringing could become extremely competitive. What if one group of ringers became too arrogant in their abilities? Might that provoke others to jealousy, even hatred? He supposed so, but to murder? He couldn't rule it out. People had been known to commit atrocious crimes for the flimsiest of reasons.

Perhaps he ought to contact the Earl of Pentelow to see if he'd found out if betting had been involved. Somehow, he couldn't believe in that either. If not greed for money, what about greed for fame? Those who bred flowers could become vicious in competing for the status that came from winning the major prize at an important show. Did anything similar exist in the odd, enclosed world of ringing changes on bells?

He could dismiss physical lust at least, he decided. Bell-ringing was an exclusively male world. Not so fast. Some men preferred to choose sexual partners from amongst their own gender. Might teaching a handsome young fellow the rudiments of handling ropes and bells stir up enough jealousy to provoke an attack on a rival? It had to be possible.

His speculations ended abruptly when he heard someone come into the room to open the shutters and set out hot water for him to wash and shave. He moved the curtain aside enough to verify that it was Molly. Excellent. He could ask her the question that had bothered him since yesterday evening.

"Molly," he called out. "In the cold weather we've had so far this spring, what do you wear to keep warm when you go out to the market?"

The fact that she answered his question without any sign of surprise said a great deal about the resilience needed by servants in Foxe's household. They never knew what their master might demand to know next.

"I'd already be wearing a thick skirt, so I'd get the good jacket you bought for me last year and button it up close. If it was very cold and windy, I'd throw my thick, woollen shawl over my head and shoulders, cross it in front and tuck the ends under my arms. That would keep me warm enough, I reckon."

"How would the wife of a shopkeeper dress?"

"She'd own a cloak of woollen cloth to put on over the rest of her clothes. Most cloaks close up at the front with ribbons or buttons and come down almost to the feet. They also have high collars to keep your neck and ears warm and slits at the side for your arms. As she walked along, she would keep her hands inside for warmth, though she'd be wearing gloves, of course."

"What would she put on her head?"

"Probably a poke bonnet with a long brim. She could see out — just — but it would shield her face from the wind."

"And a lady?"

"A lady wouldn't go out in the cold, except in a closed carriage. She'd send her poor maid instead."

Foxe joined in her laughter.

"But if she did?"

"A long cloak like the shopkeeper's wife, though of much thicker cloth, with fancy ornaments and a beautifully ruffed collar. A fashionable bonnet and fine leather gloves to protect her hands. Oh! I mustn't forget the muff. She'd have a lovely muff of rich fur and keep her hands warm in that."

The woman the children had described had worn a shawl over her head. There had been no mention of a cloak. Either a servant then, or someone from among the ranks of working people. Foxe supposed the poor would dress in the same way, if they could. Their clothes would most likely be ones handed down when they were almost worn out. Not much protection from cold or wet. It had been too dark for the children to see if the shawl had been threadbare or attacked by moths.

"Your washing and shaving things are ready, Master," Molly called out. "Shall I tell Alfred to come?"

"Give me ten minutes to rise and make my toilet. Then he can bring me my green morning gown. What's the weather like?"

"Sunny, Master. A bit warmer than of late as well."

"Maybe spring has come at last. Tell Mrs Whitbread to have my coffee and rolls ready for me. Strawberry jam today, I think, and good butter. The butter I had yesterday was on the turn, if you ask me. I have several things to do this morning, but none of them are urgent. Has Alfred collected the post?"

"I believe so, Master. He also told me Captain Brock's servant called early to see if it would be convenient for his master to call on you this morning."

"Ah, so he's back from London. Better warn Mrs Whitbread to make extra coffee and warm a few more rolls. I know the captain is very partial to her bread."

"You caught your burglar then," Brock said. "Where does that take you? Was he just a common criminal or is there more to be learned from him?"

The two friends were sitting in Foxe's library taking a late coffee.

"I had hoped there was more," Foxe said, "but it doesn't look like it. We had him locked in the Bridewell overnight and Alderman Halloran is seeing him today. Whether he'll be able to get anything useful from him remains to be seen. That's the trouble with this affair. Everyone we think is involved is telling a pack of lies."

"You didn't get to speak with the weavers?"

"Not yet."

"So what's next?"

"I'm going to confront Mrs Baker. Then I'm dining with Alderman Halloran and family. Look, Brock. Can you do something for me?"

"I'm very busy right now."

"This won't take up much of your time. All I want is for you to set some enquiries in motion amongst the shipowners and sailors in King's Lynn. James Logan's daughter, Hester, went there when she eloped. Did she stay there? Is she there now? If not, what happened to her? It's a long shot. I'm asking about events twenty-five years ago or more. Still, I have to try."

"I'll do what I can, but don't get your hopes up."

IF MRS BAKER WAS SURPRISED TO SEE MR FOXE SO SOON, SHE GAVE no sign. She offered him refreshment, which he declined, then took him into the parlour to hear what it was he wanted of her.

"When exactly did Mr James Logan die?" Foxe asked. He kept his tone as light and casual as he could.

"It must be ten years ago now, sir. If you need the exact date, I'm sure it's written down in the parish records."

"I'm sure it is, Mrs Baker, but that's not the date I want. When did your former master really die? It must have been well after that."

She didn't speak for several moments. All colour drained from her face and she sat as still and rigid as a waxwork, her eyes looking down at her hands in her lap. Foxe waited. Her mind must be in turmoil. In the end, she decided further evasion would be pointless.

"Two years ago," she whispered. "How did you guess?"

"The carvings in the library. They must have taken years to complete, even by someone working day after day. James Logan was a famous craftsman and a busy architect. He could never have made the time available."

"You're right. He was always travelling to supervise different pieces of work. That's how his condition first showed itself. He became totally lost in a part of the county he'd known since he was a child. It happened in the city too. Someone would bring him home and he'd be frightened and confused. His son covered it up by saying it was the effect of overwork, but that couldn't last."

"He became worse?"

"Sometimes too frightened to go out at all. It was as if his memory was slipping away. He wouldn't recognise close friends if he met them. He even forgot who I was sometimes. His son too. He also became unreliable."

"How?"

"He'd say and do outrageous things. Take all his clothes off and wander about naked. Ask me to show him my breasts or my legs, so he could make sure his carvings were accurate. Sit in his chair, unlace his breeches and play with himself."

"His son wouldn't have his father declared insane?"

"Absolutely not! I was never sure whether it was for love of a great man brought low by fate, or to save himself the embarrassment. Instead he came up with the idea of pretending his father had died. First he spread the word that Mr James was seriously ill. That was to account for him not going out or being about his business. Then he announced his death and had it written into the parish records. As an undertaker, it wasn't hard for him to make up a coffin, weight it down to imitate a body and arrange a suitable funeral."

"How did you manage to keep his father hidden away for … seven years, wasn't it?"

"I told you, Mr James was already frightened to go out much of the time. He suffered terrible attacks of panic too. He'd hide under a table or in a corner and declare that all kinds of dreadful creatures were trying to harm him. As his mind slipped away, he forgot almost everything. Only two things never deserted him."

"What were they?"

"His skill in carving and his memory of the Earl of Brancaster. He came to believe his own library was part of the earl's house. He also thought his old patron wanted him to decorate it with scenes from the old religions he'd written about. So long as we left him in that room with his chisels, he was happy. He was like that for seven years, as you said. Towards the end, he lost even those memories. He would hunch in a chair, staring into nothingness. He wouldn't feed himself, clean himself or do anything. When it came, death was a blessing to him as much as it was to the rest of us."

"You agreed to this deception?"

"I loved Mr James, sir. After his wife died, I was his mistress for many years. Right to the end, I could always calm him by taking him in my arms and rocking him like a baby. I would never have spoken out."

"What about Jane?"

"She didn't come to the house until a few weeks before he died. By that time, he was too much for me to deal with on my own and his son couldn't be here all the time. Mr Richard got her from the orphanage and chose her because she was dumb. That way, he said, she wouldn't be able to talk. She wouldn't have done anyway. She's a good girl."

He'd been right, but there was no pleasure in proving it. The tale was too tragic for that. Mrs Baker had hidden the secret away when

James Logan had been alive, then kept up the deception after his death. What good would it have done to speak out? Foxe imagined the household, freed from obligations to a sick man but too used to solitude to change. It explained why Richard Logan had become a recluse. It didn't help with his death though.

❧ 14 ❧

THE ALDERMAN'S HOUSE

Foxe decided to walk to the alderman's house. His mind had been whirling since he returned from talking with Mrs Baker. The fresh air would do him good. He was becoming far too lazy. No need to take a chair when his own feet were just as quick. He would also choose a different route avoiding the upper side of the Market Place, where the fish were sold.

He began by following one of the narrow lanes behind his home into St Giles Street, then down Upper Goat Lane to cross Pottergate and St Benedict's Street to St Miles Bridge. Across the river and along the street ahead until he could turn into Colegate Street by St Michael Coslany. It was further than usual, but a good deal less redolent of stale fish.

Alderman Halloran was waiting in his library. From his expression, the morning session with the burglar had not gone well.

"Damned impudent fellow," he told Foxe. "Refused at first to tell me more than his name and occupation."

"Which were?"

"Silas Napthorn, mate on the *Pretty Maid*, a collier from South Shields."

"Nothing else?"

"Nothing useful. He said you'd caught him in the act, so there was no point in him answering other questions. I asked him why he'd been back to that house several times. All he would say was that he'd heard the man who lived there was a miser, so he'd expected rich pickings. Since he was a stranger in the city, he couldn't tell which might be the best house to rob otherwise."

"True, I suppose. Still, what you've learned helps to clarify a few points. I've asked Captain Brock to assist me to find out what became of Richard Logan's sister, Hester. She eloped with a younger son from one of the gentry families her father was working for. According to Mrs Baker, she was only fifteen at the time. He was twenty-five and a wastrel in need of money. When James Logan refused to pay a dowry or advance his daughter any money from his estate, the eager suitor abandoned the girl in King's Lynn and wandered off to try his luck elsewhere."

"Has it anything to do with her father's death?"

"Will you do something for me, Alderman? I'd like you to summon one of the ringers, Mr Henry Gradnor, to come before you in your capacity as a magistrate. Make it as official as you can. If you agree, I'll be there with you, but you must conduct the questioning. Mr Gradnor is used to dealing with the law, I expect, so we need to make sure he thinks he's under suspicion of wrongdoing."

"An odd request, Foxe. Still, I'll assume you know what you're doing. When do you want this to happen?"

"Not too soon. Would Monday be suitable?"

"It will for me. I was so excited last night. Thought we'd be catching the killer. Now we're back where we started. Let's forget about this affair for a while. My wife and nieces are waiting for us to join them so dinner can be served."

"Of course, Alderman. There is more, but it'll keep until after we have dined."

Foxe had come to know Mrs Halloran well during his last investigation. She had, with great reluctance, colluded with him in letting her husband imagine his library was infested by a poltergeist. If it had not been in the cause of protecting their two beloved nieces from their uncle's justified fury, she would never have agreed to it.

The two girls were staying at the alderman's house while their parents were in China. Their father held a senior position there with the East India Company. He had only agreed to allow his wife to go with him because she insisted and he was afraid of her. He most decidedly did not think so barbarous a country a fit place for daughters. Thus there were five at the table and the conversation ranged widely. Both girls were sharp-witted and constant readers and they joined in the adults' conversation on equal terms. It was only when Mrs Halloran took them into the Withdrawing Room to drink tea that Foxe and Halloran returned to the matter of Mr Logan's death.

"We've had most of it wrong, Alderman," Foxe said. "James Logan didn't die ten years ago. He only died some two years past."

Halloran stared in amazement. "Are you sure? His son's been running that business — if business you can call it — for at least ten years. So far as everyone knows, he took over when his father died."

"That was what you were all supposed to think. The reality makes a sad story. Mrs Baker, the housekeeper, went to the family as a young maid when James Logan was making his name in the county and elsewhere. She fitted in well and moved gradually to more senior roles in the household. She was there when the daughter eloped and both times James Logan died."

"She told you all this? I still can't believe it's true."

"Only today. I knew she'd lied to me before, so I confronted her with what I had guessed. Seeing no other way out, she began to tell the truth at last."

"So how did the fake death come about?"

"James Logan was in middle age and at the height of his fame and ability when something started to go wrong with his mind. He became extremely forgetful. He would get lost in a city he had lived in all his life. He forgot to send out bills and paid accounts twice or three times. Customers who had placed orders would ask him when the work would be completed and he would deny knowing about it — even when his men were engaged on the work.

"Things got worse and worse, until it was clear he was falling into madness. By then, he could no longer be trusted to move in society or look after his affairs. All that remained was his talent for carving. He made that carving we saw in the library, starting with a block of a dark, foreign wood. In his fantasy, he thought he had been commissioned by the Earl of Brancaster to decorate the library with carvings of pagan gods and goddesses. It was his own library, of course, yet that never occurred to him.

"His son, Richard, was dismayed by his father 's descent into madness. Mrs Baker wasn't sure whether it was love of his father or embarrassment that upset him the most. Either way, he didn't want everyone knowing his father often forgot his son's name, or imagined his housekeeper was his late wife. James Logan's reputation would have been destroyed. Mrs Baker too would do anything she could to shield her master. After his wife died, she had become his mistress. She loved him dearly.

"Together, she and Richard Logan made a plan. They announced James Logan had died of a sudden apoplexy. Richard took a coffin filled with earth and sand and had it buried in the family vault. No one saw anything amiss. He was sole executor of the father's Will, so the management of everything passed into his hands."

"What did they do with James himself? They couldn't let him be seen or the plan would be ruined."

"They kept him locked in the house, away from windows looking onto the street. Mostly they kept him in the library. Mrs Baker and Richard cared for him most of the time. When they could no longer cope, they were joined by the maid Jane. To avoid visitors, Richard took on the character of a misanthrope. He invited no one to his home and avoided social events. After a while, the pose became his reality. His only outlet was his passion for change-ringing."

"Didn't his father get restless or try to escape?"

"No. Part of his madness manifested itself in irrational fears of attack by strange creatures. Mrs Baker also told me he grew terrified of clergymen. He said they wanted to have him burned for heresy. All that was left was his skill with wood. The two gave him tools and James covered the bookshelves, tables and almost anything else wooden with the most exquisite carvings, as we saw."

"He did that for more than seven years?"

"Yes. His hair and beard grew until few could have recognised him, even if he had escaped. He never tried. He had all he wanted."

"Was that why Richard neglected the business?"

"Most of his time was taken up with his father. They lived mainly on such of his father's wealth as was left. Richard mostly kept the business going to avoid suspicion, but it produced little income. It was too neglected for that. He had always been tight with money. Now he did all he could to preserve such as he had. He didn't know how long his father would live. That way of life became habitual and he didn't change it after his father died."

"This time James Logan really was buried."

"His son invented a name and represented him as a visiting stranger. A false entry went into the church register and the body was buried in an unmarked grave. After that, Richard Logan, Mrs Baker and Jane went on as before. The only difference was Richard couldn't bear to enter the parts of the house where his father had spent his time. He left everything as it was and locked the doors."

"What an amazing story! Tragic too. Still, their trick worked. James Logan is still remembered as a great craftsman and architect cut off in his prime."

"As indeed he was, but not quite in the way we thought. Can we return for a moment to Mr Gradnor. I've discovered he lied to me about what he did that night after he left the church. It may be he's fundamentally an honest, law-abiding man who has stumbled into a serious problem he can't escape. My plan is to shock the truth out of him. A summons of the kind I've asked you to make will terrify him, I hope. With enough time to fret over his predicament, he'll collapse under questioning and confess what he has been up to."

"What am I to ask him?"

"Don't worry, Alderman. I'll tell you exactly the questions to put to him."

"Very well. What are you going to do?"

Foxe seemed lost in thought. After a moment, Alderman Halloran broke the silence.

"We're in your hands, Foxe. Without you, we wouldn't have come this far. Now, another cigar? A glass of brandy? No? Very well, we'll go through to bid my nieces goodnight and take a little tea with my wife to round off the evening."

❦ 15 ❦

LIES AND DAMNED LIES

S aturday and Sunday passed quietly, at least on the outside. Foxe's mind was as active as ever and an air of abstraction confirmed to all he did not want to be disturbed. Questions would be unwelcome. Charlie, still too young to read his master's moods with accuracy, ventured to ask if he had enjoyed dinner with Alderman Halloran — as a preliminary to more engaging queries. Foxe walked past him without any sign of hearing what he said. The only time Foxe was stirred from his reverie was early on Sunday afternoon when Captain Brock came to his house.

"I knew you were in a hurry for news, Foxe," Brock said, "so I came at once. I can't stay long. For once my contacts in King's Lynn moved quickly to get the information you want. James Logan's daughter, Hester, was living there until not so long ago. She was housekeeper to a local man, who worked in the whaling business. The whaling ships go out from Lynn in spring to spend summer off the coast of Greenland. They bring their catch back in the autumn. The man she worked for was part-owner of one of the places where they boil the blubber to extract the oil. Dreadful smelly business, I believe, but profitable in good years. Anyhow, she kept house for him. She was also his mistress, though eventually they married. They had one son. All the other children died either at birth or soon after."

"You say 'was'."

"He died about three years ago. The son was apprenticed to a ship's captain in the coal trade, sailing mostly between Newcastle and London. My sources think he lives in the north country. South Shields, or somewhere like that. When the merchant Hester lived with died, she moved north to be with him. That's all there is."

"Do you think what I think? Alderman Halloran said the thief said his ship sailed out of South Shields."

"That this burglar is Hester's son? He could well be. But maybe the son got to boasting of having a rich grandfather in Norwich. One of his shipmates might have decided to use that knowledge to do a little piracy on land. Many of the coal ships call at Yarmouth on their way north or south. Most also hire a crew for only one season at a time. This could be someone who didn't get hired, so he's having to find another way to get money until next season."

Foxe nodded. "Either way, it doesn't seem to offer much in the way of an explanation for Richard Logan's death, does it? Burglary is one thing, murder quite another. If Logan had died in his house, you'd assume he'd surprised the intruder and been killed in a struggle. For a burglar to go all the way to the church to kill Logan, when the bell-ringers have been meeting there, defies common sense."

There was a knock on the door and Alfred came into the room. "There are two men asking to talk to you, Master. I have asked them to wait in the hall."

"Did they give their names?"

"Mr Ovenden and Mr Rogerstone, sir. From their clothes, they are not gentlemen. I suspect they are artisans of some kind."

"Bring them in, Alfred," Foxe said. "No, Brock, stay please, if you can. We'll talk to them together. It won't take long. What on earth can have brought them here today?"

The weavers looked scared when they came into the room. Neither was used to such grand surroundings. They held their caps in their hands and tried not to bump into anything. Foxe did not ask them to sit down.

"Well?" he said. His abrupt tone was not what they had expected. He hadn't even introduced Brock. When Foxe had met the bell-ringers the previous week, he'd taken pains to be approachable. Now he sounded haughty and irritated.

"Beg your pardon for disturbing you, sir," Ovenden began, "and you having someone with you and all. We hoped to have a private word, but if it's not convenient, we can come another time."

"You can say whatever you have to say in front of Captain Brock. He is aware of the circumstances of the murder of Mr Logan."

Brock stayed silent. From the frown on his face, he was as puzzled as the two weavers at Foxe's show of icy disinterest.

Ovenden and Rogerstone looked at one another. Neither was eager to speak. At last, Ovenden took a deep breath and began.

"Well, sir. It's like this, you see. We wasn't quite as honest with you as we should have been last Friday. That is to say—"

"You lied to me. I am aware of that."

Rogerstone's face had lost most of its colour and he'd started to sweat. You could smell it. Ovenden battled on, trying to be deferential, but only succeeding in sounding slimy.

"That's a harsh way of putting it, sir. What I mean to say is—"

"Then say it. You both told me you had gone home after the practice. You, Rogerstone, said you had done so directly. You, Ovenden, said you went into The White Swan for twenty minutes or so, then walked home alone. Both of you lied. You went back to the ringing chamber, didn't you?"

Brock thought Rogerstone was going to faint. Ovenden was made of somewhat sterner stuff, but even he was white-faced and shaking.

"We did, sir," Ovenden managed to gasp, "But Logan was alive and well when we went in and when we came out. We swear that's true! I did go to The White Swan, only it was a little later than I let you believe. We both wanted to talk to Logan, you see. Persuade him to give up being Tower Captain and drop this mad notion of repeating 'The Bloody Peal'."

It took several minutes to get Ovenden to give a coherent explanation of what that strange term meant. Eventually, Foxe grasped that the arcane art of change-ringing advanced by teams of ringers proved in practice what had before been but mathematical theory. The goal was to ring the bells in a set number of different sequences, one after the other, changing on each sounding of the bells. It was not too hard — if you were mathematically inclined — to calculate the total number of such unique sequences that were possible, given a specific number of bells. What was much harder was to work out how to produce a system that would be feasible in a church tower.

A bell could only change its position in the sequence by one place each time it rang. Either that or stay where it was while the others changed. You had to calculate precisely which bell must change with which others and when it must stand in the same place. If you got it wrong, the ringers would either repeat a sequence or return to the starting point before the intended sequence was complete. The only way you could prove to the world — at least, the world of fellow enthusiasts — that you'd done it right was ringing a peal.

"It were a while ago now, sirs," Ovenden explained, "in March, 1738. The Mancroft ringers rang a peal of 12,600 changes. There's a board in the tower what records the event. Eleven ringers there were. Two of them shared ringing the tenor bell, since that's the heaviest."

"Why is it called The Bloody Peal?" Foxe asked.

"From the state of the men's hands at the end. It took eight and a quarter hours, non-stop."

"Mr Logan wanted to do that again?"

"He did, sir. Mad on it he was. You see, some people outside the city tried to throw doubt on the achievement. They said there must have been someone calling out sequences from a sheet. That's not allowed, you see. Cheating. Each ringer must remember what he needs to do. Others said there were extra people taking over from time to time, only their names weren't recorded. Logan took all this very badly. His scheme was to prove it had been done by doing it again."

"And you others didn't agree?"

"It was a fine idea, but terrible hard work. Most of us has to earn our living. We can't spare the practice time you'd need to stand even a chance of getting it right. Logan had been Tower Captain for years and was used to having his own way. He swore that, so long as he was captain, we would do as he wanted. I suppose we could have asked for a vote of the ringers on whether he should stay on as Captain, but no one dared cross him. Of late he's been real foul tempered. He's also a fine conductor of peals and has served the band for nigh on forty years. In the end, Rogerstone here and I were deputed to ask him to step aside, voluntary like. We was to tell him that, if he didn't, there would be a vote and he would likely be told to go."

"What did he say to that?"

"Swore terrible. Said that we could have twenty votes and he'd still be captain. You wouldn't credit his temper when he's roused, sir. He threatened to send us all packing and recruit a whole new band. Claimed the Coslany men would be mad keen to come to Mancroft. All he needed was to show them the way he'd composed the peal. None of us had ever been shown that, sirs. He'd never explained any of his composing, nor described the principles even. If the Coslany men knew and we didn't, it would be a sore blow to our pride."

"That's it? You tried to reason with him and he dismissed you out of hand?"

"Aye. I were so upset I needed a drink. That's why I went into the Swan. Rogerstone here went straight home, didn't you?"

Rogerstone nodded. He hadn't spoken the whole time the two men had been in the room. He was hiding something, not just from them but from Ovenden too. Foxe was sure of that. Given the man's timid nature, it might be nothing any other person would consider hiding. Foxe felt sure a few more days of continual nervousness, followed by some kindness, would shake it out of him.

"Right. You can go back to your homes. I can't see why you didn't tell me this the first time I spoke to you."

"We was afraid of being accused of the killing, sir."

"Nothing has changed. I still only have your word that everything happened as you say. You've lied once, so why should I believe you this time?"

"But it's the truth! We swears it!" Ovenden was near the end of his tether. Rogerstone's sweat was making the whole room smell rank. Foxe seemed as unconcerned as he had been at the start.

"You've said what you came to say. Be off now and let me think about it. You bell-ringers wanted me to find Mr Logan's killer. That's what I mean to do, whoever it is."

After the men had gone, Foxe got up and opened the door to let the smell of fear escape. Brock stood up as well.

"You were damned hard on the fellow," he said. "I've never seen you like that before. I was almost afraid of you myself."

Foxe grinned. "Play-acting, Brock. I'm sure those two came here with a prepared tale. I had to tip them off balance for the truth to come out. They expected a polite hearing, so I provided the opposite. My belief is that we got most, maybe all, of the truth out of Ovenden. Rogerstone I'm not so sure about. What do you think?"

"He's so afraid he can hardly stand up. I agree with you, there's more to be extracted from him, so long as he doesn't try to run away."

"I don't think he'll do that. If that appealed he'd have done it by now. I'll let him fret for a day or so, then call him back to hear his confession. In the meantime, I'll send Charlie to tell the street children to watch him. If he does try to leave the city, they'll warn me and I'll send the constables to arrest him. I'm attending the alderman tomorrow morning. He's summoned the other bell-ringer, Mr Gradnor, to answer questions. Why don't you come along? I'm sure he wouldn't mind. It'll save me telling you everything second hand."

"Sorry, Foxe. I agreed to meet Lady Julia tomorrow. She's buying some new outfits for her travels and wants my opinion."

"Ominous, Brock. Very ominous. When a woman wants your opinion on her clothes, there can be only one result."

"Nonsense! I've explained that to you before."

"I didn't believe you then either. Off you go! Don't keep the lady waiting tomorrow. You've got the best of this bargain, Brock. Lady Julia is much better looking than the alderman."

❧ 16 ❧

CONFESSIONS

onday afternoon came. Mr Henry Gradnor, factor and bell-ringer, arrived and was shown into the parlour of Alderman Halloran's house, where Foxe and the alderman were waiting. With him he brought an odour Foxe placed as a compound of expensive pomade, common tobacco and trepidation. Despite his fine clothes and assumed swagger, Mr Gradnor was scared. He looked like a novice actor thrust into the leading role on the first night of a play. Worse, on the night when the manager of the company had invited his most influential friends and patrons to admire the latest production. He had learned his lines and practiced his moves. Sadly, he suspected he possessed neither the skill nor the confidence to play the part required.

It started to go wrong from his opening lines. "Why have you summoned me here, sir? I am a busy man with a great deal to do. My business cannot be set aside on some minor matter."

Alderman Halloran allowed a lengthy pause before he replied. "I dare say I am a good deal busier than you are, Mr Gradnor, and even less willing to waste my time on minor matters. Since you have, as yet, no knowledge of why I wish to speak with you, it would be more sensible to assume my reasons are not trivial ones."

Mr Gradnor swallowed hard, then made another ill-judged attempt to seize the initiative.

"I meant no disrespect, Alderman. I am here, as you see. For what reason I cannot imagine."

"Can you not, sir? I find that hard to believe. A person who is present in company with a man murdered soon afterwards must surely expect to be questioned on the matter."

"He was alive when I left with the others. We all went home directly."

"That is not true, is it, Mr Foxe?"

"Not at all, Alderman. Two have already admitted to returning to the ringing chamber. There were others, doubtless including Mr Gradnor here."

Mr Gradnor's face had become a most unbecoming shade of yellowish-green. Foxe could see sweat on his brow. It would not be long before the fellow must either collapse or beg for mercy.

"Really? I did not know that."

"Obviously not," Halloran said. "You would have taken more care not to be observed." Though this was not exactly a lie, it was a shrewd move and threw Mr Gradnor completely off balance.

"But no one could have seen me go back. No one!" He was too rattled by the alderman's remark to realise what he had admitted. The end came almost at once.

"Why would I wish to speak to Mr Logan in private?" he said. "What would be the purpose in doing so?"

It was Foxe who struck the final blow. "To talk about the money, of course," he said as if it were entirely obvious.

The outcome was like a mountain peak crashing down in an earthquake. Gradnor gave an inarticulate gasp of horror and burst into tears.

"I am ruined! Totally ruined! My wife and children will be put in the workhouse, all because of me. Oh Merciful Lord, let me die now! Let me die!"

It took Foxe and the alderman several minutes, and a good deal of brandy, to restore Mr Gradnor to coherent speech. By the end, his wig had fallen off and his face, hands and the front of his waistcoat were so wet with tears he could have been out in a thunderstorm.

"Now, sir," Halloran said after a while, "pull yourself together and tell us the truth this time. You make a very poor liar. All your evasions have done is raise what are probably needless suspicions. Come. You will feel a good deal better afterwards, I assure you."

Mr Gradnor's tale was not especially surprising. Essentially, he was an honest and law-abiding fellow, forced into a position he found unmanageable.

As the purse-holder for the ringing team, he was in charge of a substantial amount of cash. Demands on the balance were low; small charges for maintenance and the occasional payment for a member who fell sick and could not work for a short period. Seeing the balance lying fallow, as it were, he decided he would appear a fine fellow in the eyes of the rest of the team if he set the unused amount to work. He would hold back enough for anticipated expenditure, plus a small reserve. The rest he would use to gain interest. Thus, when he next presented his annual accounting, he would be able to show an additional credit as the direct result of his stewardship.

Unfortunately, he had too little experience in the ways of investors. He was not a wealthy man. As a factor, his task was to receive payments for his clients, deduct his commission, pay any agreed bills and forward the balance. His only contact with credit or debt came when they instructed him to use certain amounts of income to meet obligations they had entered into on their own. His was not a business that existed on credit.

Being a novice in the field, therefore, he fell into the hands of those who saw him as ripe to be plucked. They persuaded him to use the money he held for the ringers to make a series of loans offering high interest. For two or three months, all went as planned, then the debtors and his money disappeared overnight.

All was not quite lost. He still had funds enough to cover normal expenditure. Being an honest man, he was determined to make good what he had lost. All it needed was time. He did not have the means to make restitution at once, but he was sure he could do so within a year or two at the most.

Then Mr Logan went to him and demanded two hundred pounds at once to buy new sets of bell ropes and have the bearings on all the bells thoroughly checked and lubricated in advance of his planned rerun of the 'Bloody Peal'.

The money wasn't there. That was what he had gone back to tell Logan that evening. To confess to his folly and plead for silence and time to make all good. Any suggestion of financial trouble or wrong-doing would destroy his business.

"What did Mr Logan say?"

"He flew into one of his terrible rages and cursed me soundly. In the end, he gave me two days to produce the money. If I could not, he would tell the others and the rest of the city as well. Two days! I begged and pleaded, but he was adamant. He was a rich man, Alderman. He could easily have loaned me the money I needed. I would have paid him back, even if I had to live on gruel and wear my clothes until they fell into rags. He would not hear of it."

"And you could not raise the money any other way?"

"Not in two days. I dared not approach anyone in Norwich for fear that news of my losses would leak out. My only hope would have been to go to London and try my luck there."

"So what did you do?"

"I went home in the greatest misery I had ever felt. All night I lay awake, but could find no solution. You can imagine my feelings the next day when the news reached me that Logan was dead. At first, I assumed it was a natural death. After, when I heard it was murder, I was terrified in case I had been seen returning to the ringing chamber. If so, I would surely be suspected. I couldn't even be sure Mr Logan had told no one of my secret. That's why I did not come to the practice where you were to be present, Mr Foxe. I was afraid I would give myself away. When your summons reached me, Alderman, I felt I was already called into the dock to stand trial for my life."

"Logan was alive when you left him?" Foxe asked.

"I swear it! I did not lay a finger on him. I can see him now, his face mottled red with fury and his hands clenched into fists. I was coming between him and the peal which obsessed him. If murder was to be done, it would have been him who did me to death."

They had sent Mr Gradnor away, agreeing to disclose nothing of what he had told them unless justice demanded it. Then the alderman and Foxe discussed what they had learned.

"Do you believe him?" Alderman Halloran asked.

"Yes, I do. He's a fool for sure, but I cannot see him resorting to murder. Too timid. Too law-abiding. He had a strong motive for keeping Mr Logan silent, so I may be wrong. Had Logan been struck down by a blow to the head, say, I might assume Gradnor had lashed out in fear and anger, killing him by mistake. You don't push a man to the floor and cut his throat unless you're set on killing."

"I agree. Mr Gradnor isn't clear of all suspicion, but he doesn't rank high as a suspect. We can also ignore the thief you took in Logan's house."

"I wonder. I'm a stubborn man. No, I shall bide my time a little longer yet, Alderman. I lack enough ammunition yet to break down his resistance. I must also tell you what I learned yesterday from Captain Brock.

"James Logan's daughter, Hester, eloped and was abandoned, as I told you. It seems she stayed in Lynn and managed to find work as a housekeeper. In time, she became her employer's mistress as well. They had several children who died young. Apart, that is, for a son, who was apprenticed to the sea. The last anyone heard of Hester Logan, her employer had died and she'd left the town to join her son in South Shields."

"South Shields! Could this thief be the son?"

"Maybe, but why come back now? There's no reason to suggest he or his mother are in desperate need of money. It's common for masters to leave their housekeepers a bequest in their Will, especially if they've been sharing the same bed. The son's in steady employment, probably well on his way to getting command of a ship. Why turn to burglary? Brock thinks it's more likely a former shipmate heard Hester's son boasting about having a rich grandfather in Norwich. He might have asked the man's name and planned to pay him a visit when he could. Even if the real Silas Napthorn is mate on the *Pretty Maid*, this might not be him. We could have caught a common criminal, who decided to use his name as a disguise. Napthorn might be far off on the high seas, for all we know."

"BLOOD AND GORE
EVERYWHERE!"

Foxe was not aware of the way his behaviour changed during one of his investigations. At the start, he would appear full of energy, light-hearted, even joyful. Then, as setbacks arose, he sank into dejections and frustration. Those were the times when his staff would decide the best place to be was as far away from the master as possible. The breakthrough was signalled by rapid changes of mind, unfathomable questions and such a withdrawal of attention from other matters that Alfred had once reported that the master had been standing and staring at a featureless wall for all of fifteen minutes.

Thus it was that when, after breakfast next morning, Foxe rang and told Molly to send Mrs Dobbins, his housekeeper, to him, the poor woman was almost too nervous to respond.

Foxe was staring out of the window when Mrs Dobbins entered. He didn't greet her or turn around. Instead, he asked all his questions facing the other way. Did she hold all his household keys? She did. Had she ever known the owner of a house to demand that his housekeeper surrender all keys to him, yet keep her position?

"Never, Master. To be honest with you, I can't imagine any self-respecting housekeeper would stay in such circumstances. It would be as much as to say she was no longer judged trustworthy."

"That is what I thought, Mrs Dobbins. You may go."

Back in the kitchen, Mrs Dobbins told the others that things were happening and they'd better be ready for anything.

"Never even looked at me," she said. "All he wanted to know was about household keys. I couldn't make head nor tail of it. We're in for a lively time, I reckon."

After breakfast, Foxe neglected his usual routine. Instead, he remained shut in his library for several hours. Everyone could hear him pacing up and down, swearing loudly from time to time. He asked for no refreshment and all were too frightened to offer any. Even Alfred, who was usually the most robust in dealing with Mr Foxe's moods, remained below stairs.

It was perhaps a quarter past three, with the day still bright and chill and the promise of a cold night ahead, when Foxe left his self-imposed isolation and stepped through the connecting door into his shop.

"Who found the body?" he said, without the slightest preamble. "Why has no one told me?"

"I can tell you that," Mrs Crombie said. "He's been trying to cadge pints by telling his story ever since. It was the old verger, Mr Pither. He came in next morning to open up and found the door that leads to the ringing chamber still open. You'll find him in the church most days. I don't know where he lives, but he hangs around the church most of the time. He must be seventy or more, so he may not have anyone to talk to at home. I'd better warn you. Once he finds someone to listen to him, he's impossible to stop."

"I'll go and find him," Foxe said. "Charlie, run to the alderman's house and leave a message that I need to know the state of Logan's corpse. I know his throat was cut, but had he suffered any other injuries? How much blood was around the body? Will the alderman please find that out for me as soon as possible?"

With that, he left.

"Can you imagine being married to a man like that?" Miss Benfield said, after Foxe had gone.

"Yes," her cousin replied. "I rather think I can."

NATHANIEL PITHER, FOR THIRTY YEARS AND MORE THE VERGER OF
St. Peter Mancroft, was as eager to describe his discovery of Mr
Logan's body as Mrs Crombie had suggested. The problem was to stop
him adding embellishments to make his story more dramatic. Foxe
reckoned he must have recited it so many times even he could no
longer tell fact from fiction. It was going to take him longer than he
hoped to sort out what the old man had seen with his own eyes from
all the things he thought should have been there. These ranged from a
furtive shadow slipping out of the church as he arrived, to Logan's
hands clutching the wall in his dying agony.

He declared at the start that there was "blood everywhere from
floor to ceiling." Since the ceiling in question must, he agreed, be at
least fifteen feet from the floor, this was set aside. So was the idea that
Logan had reeled around the ringing chamber, spraying blood and gore
"inches thick" over every surface below head height. After more
tedious questioning and grudging admissions, it was established that
most of the blood had been under the body itself. If this corresponded
with what Alderman Halloran could tell him of the medical findings,
Foxe might have come within range of the truth.

Even Mr Pither found himself unable to invent a knife that had not
been there, so that point was swiftly agreed. No knife or other blade
found. Next Foxe asked what clothing was on the body.

Logan had been wearing his coat, buttoned up, as if he had been about
to leave when death claimed him. He wore no wig and his hat was lying a
little aside from his body. It might have been in his hand when he fell.
After so much rationality, Foxe felt it was only polite to allow Mr Pither to
claim the man's face had been frozen in an expression of nameless horror.
"As if he'd looked on Satan hisself," the man had said. Since they had
already agreed that the body was found face down, and Mr Pither denied
that he had moved it, the impossibility of seeing the dead man's expression should have occurred to him. However, Foxe's exclamations of well-
stimulated horror at this description restored the verger to good humour.

Pither knew little else of use. He had not noticed anyone else in the church when he arrived. Nothing had been dropped on the spiral stairs or elsewhere to indicate persons unknown had been loitering there. The old man contorted his face with the effort of trying to dream up yet more 'observations' to keep his visitor talking, but to no avail. After barely thirty minutes, Foxe left.

Back at home, he ate his dinner in total silence, drank two glasses of excellent port as if they had contained water, and returned to his study. Then the pacing began again. This time, however, the swearing was absent and only a low muttering could be heard in its place. It sounded like an actor trying to learn his lines. Once, a great cry of "Fool!" startled everyone. Once there came a stamping of feet. Then silence. No one heard their master go up to bed. When Molly took the washing things and hot water up the next morning, the reason became clear. The master was not in his room and his bed had not been slept in. They found him in the library, still asleep in his chair.

Due to this unconventional start to the day, Alderman Halloran arrived the next morning while Foxe was still taking his breakfast. Being involved in Foxe's investigation was exciting. He'd done better than consult the coroner's records, he'd spoken to the coroner himself.

"I wasn't impressed by the man," he told Foxe. "Far too self-important. He's just a local lawyer. Gives himself airs and graces as if he's a major part of the judicial system. Be that as it may. He did a superficial job on Logan's inquest. Because the man had his throat cut, he barely bothered to read the medical report beyond the minimum details of cause of death."

"Damn," Foxe said. "I was hoping to find if Logan had suffered any other injuries."

"He had. It took a while, but I persuaded the coroner to call for the detailed notes from the medical examiner. Aside from the obvious wound, Mr Logan had received a heavy blow to his chest, resulting in a fair amount of bruising. There was also a long cut on his left side, probably done by a knife blade. His waistcoat and shirt were cut in the same place."

"Anything else?"

"No. That's all. There was no examination made of his internal organs. Cause of death was obvious, you see. Oh yes, his eyes were tightly shut and his hands clenched, not around his throat but on his chest. He'd fallen on them."

"Odd. You'd expect the poor man to have clutched his throat in a dying attempt to breathe."

"The surgeon who did the examination also wrote that the upper part of Logan's shirt was soaked in blood, but there was relatively little elsewhere. None on his hands or shoulders, for example, and very little above his chin."

"That's even stranger. It sounds as if he must have been face down on the floor when someone came from behind and cut his throat. Had he been knocked down by the blow that had bruised his chest? You'd expect someone hit hard from in front to fall on his back, not forward onto his face. I can't make head nor tail of it."

"Perhaps he did fall backwards, then twisted onto his front to attempt to get up again, but his attacker forced him back down before wielding the knife. It wasn't found, by the way. The killer must have taken it away."

"I thought the killer must have been well splashed with blood. Now I suppose he might not have been. If Logan was face down and the murderer behind him, he could have escaped without much blood on him."

"Perhaps so."

They discussed it for a little longer, then gave up. Neither could see any obvious answers to most of their concerns.

"You've done a wonderful job, Alderman, and I thank you most sincerely. Since you're here, I ought to tell you about the visit I had from Mr. Ovenden and Mr. Rogerstone, if you can spare the time."

Foxe described the visit of the two weavers and what they had told him — or rather, what one had said on their behalf. He didn't go into detail on 'The Bloody Peal'. Alderman Halloran wasn't a man who was comfortable with whatever he didn't understand. He just said Logan had been trying to force the band of ringers to do something most of them felt was too time-consuming and difficult. When they tried to make him see sense, he flew into a rage and refused to listen.

"But Logan was alive when they left him?"

"So they said. We only have their word for that. I think Ovenden can be trusted to have told the truth this time. Rogerstone is still lying, in my opinion. He could easily have left Ovenden heading for a much-needed jug of ale and doubled back into the church. Still, he's such a frightened man I'm sure he'll have to confess the truth before long. I made sure I pointed out that nothing either had said would free them from the suspicion of murder. Now I'll wait for his nerves to do the work for me."

"You're a cruel man at times, Foxe, as well as devious."

"Not half as cruel as a man who slits another man's throat, Alderman."

"What's next?"

"Being as patient as I can be. I'm hoping a week in the Castle gaol will convince the supposed Silas Napthorn to be less arrogant when I choose to visit him. In the meantime, I'll go back and talk to Mrs Baker again. See if she can tell me any more about Hester Logan. If I let Napthorn understand I know a good deal about the history of that unhappy woman, I may be able to prove he knows far less and force him to change his story. If he is her son, talking about her in a sympathetic way may loosen his tongue."

"You're still on that track? I thought we'd agreed the thief and the murderer had to be two separate people?"

"They do, Alderman, but which two? I've sent word to the warden of the gaol to expect me after noon. If he does as I've asked, he'll have Napthorn waiting for me in a cell by himself. I'm certain he must have been one of the mysterious visitors that evening after the others had left. Unfortunately, he's the only one who can confirm this — if he's willing, of course."

"Good luck, then. Perhaps a few days in that hellhole will have softened his resolve to stay silent. He's got nothing to lose by confessing. He's already bound to get a death sentence for what he stole."

"He's got nothing to gain either, which is a great shame. He may believe that, as a thief, he'll avoid the hangman and be transported. If you add murder to the charges, the noose seems inevitable. If he did commit murder, that is."

"Do you believe he didn't?"

"I've got this strange notion in my mind that we've missed the whole point of this murder from the start. If I'm right, I can't see why Napthorn should have wanted to kill Logan at all. It would have been more to his advantage for the man to be alive."

"But if he didn't kill him, who did?"

"That, I do not know — yet."

18

"THAT HELLHOLE"

Monday. The sun warm enough for people to stop whatever they were doing and spend a moment or so with their faces turned towards the sky. As the clocks struck noon, Foxe threaded his way across the Market Place between the lines of stalls, many thronged with customers and idlers. Along the way, he stopped to buy a posy of sweet-smelling flowers and herbs from a market woman. He would want some refuge from the persistent odour you got in any prison.

He had kept dress as drab as he could. No watch or quizzing glass either. Temptations to light fingers inside the prison were best avoided. Even his walking stick was a plain one without any fine metal ornaments. Earlier, he had gone to the market and hired two brawny fellows to accompany him and make sure he went in and out safely. Few gentlemen were ever seen within the walls of the prison, not even those charged with its operation. The governor was known to be a humane man, as far as that was possible, but many of the warders were little better than brutes. Violence was likely to break out at any time. Human beings kept locked up for years at a time in filthy, insanitary conditions, fed barely enough to stay alive, were not to be trusted too close to you.

The men he had hired were waiting at the doorway to the castle. Even they looked nervous. Foxe's shilling had been temptation enough to take the job on in the sunshine of the market. Now, under the massive outer walls of the old castle, they were beginning to regret it. Neither had entered the place before, but many tales circulated about the filth and horrors to be found within.

As they passed through the wall and began to climb the pathway up the mound towards the keep, Foxe could smell the prisoners. A horrifying stench of too many people confined in too small a space without adequate water or sanitation. Norwich Castle was still an impressive fortification, despite many decades of neglect. By setting it on a great mound above both city and river, its builders fully intended to intimidate all who approached. Foxe knew the massive keep was little more than a shell, filled with tumbledown buildings for the prisoners. Yet he could never see it without the hairs on his neck responding to such grim and threatening bulk.

They were not on their own in approaching the prison gateway. A thin trickle of other people went with them, mostly women, carrying bundles. The warders were supposed to make sufficient plain food available to the prisoners to keep them alive and well until either trial, transfer to the prison hulks to await transportation to the American colonies or execution. In practice, everything had a price, even survival. Local prisoners were lucky. Their families could come in and out with food and fresh clothing, so long as they paid the warder's toll. The rest fared as best they could, the women selling their bodies and the men fighting and stealing over whatever was unguarded.

Since Foxe was known to be a gentleman and a friend of men in high places, the Chief Warder received his party with fawning expressions of duty. He had also taken care to give the governor and chief warder tangible expressions of his gratitude for their assistance; expressions which bore golden smiles and the king's portrait. A room was ready for him which was almost clean, with a chair the turnkey polished with his own handkerchief before inviting Foxe to be seated. They had even made an effort to clean Napthorn up before bringing him in. As a stranger, without relatives or friends in the city, he'd already have exhausted such money as he had in getting food and something better to drink than rainwater from the buckets left to catch the leaks.

Foxe told his escort to stand outside the door and see no one entered. "Mr Napthorn," he began, once the two were alone. "I have come to hear your story. You have nothing to gain by staying silent."

"Nor by speaking neither. You caught me, fair and square, entering a house and trying to make off with what I could steal. My story, as you put it, will not change any of that, nor save me from a death sentence. I've not committed murder, sir. Thief I may be, but I've killed no man."

"I believe you. Let me help you loosen your tongue by telling you of some of the facts I have uncovered. If I am correct, you have only to agree with me. If I am not, it will hardly matter whether you speak out or not."

"I've said all I'm willing to say."

"We will see. It's my belief that you are the child of Richard Logan's sister, who I believe is called Hester. You came to Norwich either at her suggestion or because of stories she told you of her childhood here. You knew — or thought you did — that her brother was a rich man. You hoped to persuade him to send you home with a sizeable amount of money. The day that he died, you went to his house, but he refused to speak with you. It was clear he either didn't believe you had any ties of blood to him or didn't care."

Napthorn was silent. Foxe waited a moment, then continued.

"Somehow you learned that Mr Logan would attend a meeting of the bell-ringers that evening. Either that, or you waited outside and followed him. Your plan was to come upon him where he could not shut you out. Then he would be forced to listen. When the other ringers left, you went inside and tried again to speak with him. He rebuffed you again, so you decided to return to his house, break in and steal what he would not give you willingly. What you believed was your due."

Still silence.

"There must have been some reason for you to come to Norwich now," Foxe said. "If I understood, I might be able to help. If you stay silent, your mother will never see you again and be left to fend for herself."

"My mother is sick. There, will that satisfy you? Sick and in want. Wouldn't any son want to help in such a situation? Now, I will say no more."

"I will strike a bargain with you, Napthorn. Tell me what I wish to know and I will send your mother enough money each year to let her live in modest comfort. I will also do my best to let you have word of her for as long as you both live."

"From your own pocket, I suppose." Napthorn's words came out in an ugly sneer.

"From my own pocket. What is your response? Do we have a bargain or not?"

"How do I know I can trust you?"

"You don't, any more than I know in advance I can trust what you tell me. If a man knows what will happen is certain, what need is there for trust?"

"Fine words!"

"Think them over before you refuse. What have you to lose by this bargain? Refuse it and your mother will descend further into want. Accept it and there is a chance of easing her final days. That's what you say that you intended by coming here. Even if you cannot be by her side, she will not face a future of misery. She will know you were thinking of her and her well-being, even if you must end your life as a felon. Is that not worth a few honest words?"

Foxe's words struck home. Of a sudden, Napthorn abandoned his silence. Now he was eager to explain himself.

"I was desperate," he said. "That devil and his father drove my mother from her home years before. Forced her from a life of ease and left her to struggle on her own to survive. Eventually, she married a good man, well able to support her until sickness came upon him. After he died, I sent all the money I could back home from the meagre wages I earned on the colliers. My mother has suffered years of hardship, sir. Much of my father's money was lost when his business failed.

I am all she has, the only surviving son ... and now I have failed her too."

"You must have known her father and brother had cut her off all those years before. Since that time, it seems, she had no further contact with either. What made you think her brother would change his attitude? You knew her father was dead?"

"She had read it in an old newspaper, years after it happened. Her brother, Richard Logan, would have inherited a good deal of money, she told me. Money that by all natural justice he should have shared with her."

"But not under the law, presumably. I was told all his father's wealth descended to him."

"What is the law? We're talking of brother and sister. Would you believe any Christian man would deny his own sister a small part of his wealth to comfort her at the end of her life? That is exactly what her brother did, sir. I hated him for it."

"Yet you say you left him in the tower, alive and well."

"I did. That I swear."

"Someone ended his life that evening and in that place. Nothing would be simpler than to reason that you, driven by the hatred you admit, did away with your uncle, Richard Logan."

"Believe it if you like. I tell you it isn't true, but I have no way to prove my words. I will hang anyway, so it makes no odds. I have failed in what I set myself to do. I will never see my mother again, nor be able to bring her comfort in her final days. For that, my death seems a fitting punishment."

Napthorn couldn't sit still any longer. He jumped up, went to the wall of the room and beat his fists upon it. Then he threw back his head and let out a howl of misery. That brought the turnkey and Foxe's bodyguards running in.

It took some while to convince them Foxe was in no danger and that the shackles the turnkey had snatched up were not needed. Reluctantly, all three left again, assuring Foxe that they would stay within call, should Napthorn turn violent. Foxe took a small flask from his pocket and offered it to Napthorn. When the prisoner found it contained good brandy, he drank it down eagerly. After that, with a great sigh, he went on with his story.

"You've already guessed most of it, sir. My mother was James Logan's only daughter. When she was fifteen, a wretch seduced her and persuaded her to elope with him. They went to King's Lynn, from where he sent word to her father that he would marry her in return for a dowry of two thousand pounds. When his offer was refused, he abandoned her. Went off to find an easier, and hopefully richer, victim, I imagine. My mother told me she expected to return to Norwich in disgrace and face severe punishment for her foolishness. What she did not expect was that her father would disown her in his anger and her older brother encourage such severity.

"I will not weary you with the details of her life after that. She was forced to take work as a servant for a time. She spent a period in the workhouse. Eventually she married a good man, who did his best to make her happy. That was my father, sir, Elias Napthorn. Unfortunately, he began to suffer long periods of sickness. It prevented him from working for weeks at a time and ruined his business. Five years ago, his sickness proved fatal.

"By then I was working as an able seaman on a collier, sailing between South Shields and London. My mother left her house in King's Lynn, gathered together what little my father had left her, and came north to be with me. It must have been around the same time she learned her father had died years earlier. She hoped he might have softened his attitude to her. Left her a small bequest or annuity. If so, her brother had never sought her out. I believe she wrote to him to ask him if anything was due to her, but he ignored her letter. Richard had always loved money more than anything else, she told me. When I came to Norwich, everyone said the man was a notorious miser."

"Why did you come now?"

"Alas, sir, my mother grew sick, as I told you. I thought if he knew this, her brother might give her something out of pity, to help tide her over, as they say. I never asked for more than that. I send her what I can, for I am the mate of a fine ship. I had hoped to be a captain soon, had I not fallen into this evil pass. Then I could turn my back for ever on Logan, as he and his father had done to us."

"You asked for your mother."

"I did, sir. I have no claim on him."

"Even so, he refused you."

"Utterly. I explained who I was and why I had come and he shouted at me like a madman. Called my mother filthy names — slut and whore were the least of them. According to him, she had so dishonoured the family all those years ago that she should not have a farthing. If she died sick and in poverty, it was what she deserved."

"I was told he had developed a vile temper in recent years."

"That is too weak a description. Do you wonder that I hated him? When I heard some man had ended his life, I was glad. If anyone deserved to die, it was Richard Logan. The rest you know. The first time I got into the house, I found almost all the doors locked. I am not really a burglar. I had never done such a thing before, so was bound to make a mess of it. I made too much noise and roused the servants. Rather than be caught, I fled."

"Yet you stayed in Norwich."

"As I told you, I was desperate not to return home empty handed. I reasoned that I was a stranger and no one knew who I was. Only Mr Logan knew I had gone to the church tower and spoken to him there."

"So you tried again to break into the house."

"I did. The man was dead. Now the only way to get anything was by taking it. If I could take enough to raise a good price, I could rejoin my ship and nobody would ever know what I had done."

"Was your ship at Great Yarmouth? I thought you said she sailed to London."

"We suffered some damage to the rudder in a storm. The captain put into Great Yarmouth for repairs. Within a day or so now the ship will be ready to seek favourable winds and sail north again."

"That is all?"

"It is, sir. Word had reached me the servants had left the house, since its master would never return. When I saw that window ajar, I thought my luck had changed. I should have known better."

"Let me be clear. Mr Richard Logan was alive when you left him?"

"Alive and furious. If anyone was ready to do murder, it was him. That was partly why I left. He snatched up a stick someone had left there and was trying to strike me with it. I drew a knife I always carried and threatened him with it. Even then he tried to come at me, so that my knife caught in his coat and I dropped it."

"You gashed his side. Not enough to do him any great harm, but enough to show. What did you do with your knife?"

"I must have left it behind when I ran. He was lashing out at me with that great stick. If I had bent down to pick it up, he would have brought the stick down on my head and killed me."

As he left the prison, Foxe made sure to give Napthorn a few pennies to buy food and clean linen. Not too much, or the others would set on the man and steal it. He could arrange with Charlie for some of the street children to take him further supplies from time to time. They went everywhere. Few even noticed them. Then he hurried back to Alderman Halloran's house, hoping to catch him before he went out visiting or on business.

⬥

"What an amazing tale," the alderman said as they sat in his library. Foxe had met him at his door and turned him back to hear the latest news. "Do you believe the fellow?"

"I do," Foxe said. "Everything he told me fits. He's acted stupidly, and he'll suffer the penalty, but he's not really a criminal. I'll ask to speak on his behalf when he comes to trial. It may do no good, but I have to try."

"The man's an experienced seaman too. Tell you what, Foxe. I'll have a word with the mayor. See if he'd be willing to write privately to the judge in the case. Napthorn should be allowed to serve out his sentence in the navy rather than be executed or sent to the colonies. I've known that happen. So ... what are you going to do next?"

"I wanted to talk with Rogerstone again today. I sent him a message, but he begged to be excused until tomorrow. Says he has a large weaving order he has to get finished. He'll be at his loom until nightfall."

"I hope he's not planning to abscond."

"So do I. I've sent the street children to watch him. They have their own methods of delaying him while they send word to me. Instead, I'm going to talk to Mrs Baker. The trouble with this investigation has been the same from the start, Alderman. Everyone tells me nothing but lies."

"Even Mrs Baker?"

"Especially Mrs Baker. She has a sharp mind and ample time to concoct plausible tales. Now I plan to get the truth from her too. If I hadn't been such a blockhead, her falsehoods and evasions would have ended long before now."

"I'm sure you'll smoke her out, Foxe. She can't be more cunning than you are."

"Let us hope not, or we'll never come to the truth."

"I should also tell you that I have written to the attorney, Mr Bonnard, about certain debt obligations to be met before the bequests in Richard Logan's Will can be paid. If I am right, and I believe I am, he will find several bequests made under the father's Will that have never been discharged. I'm no lawyer, but I don't think the passage of time will have changed the duty of the executors of that Will to carry out the deceased's last wishes."

"Are you saying these bequests are outstanding and must still be paid? What are they?"

"I don't know precisely, Alderman. That's why I've asked Mr Bonnard to obtain sight of the original Will. If they are specific sums, they will surely count as unpaid debts, perhaps even with accrued interest. If they are annuities, they may need to be paid from the date the Will was falsely proved. By advancing the date of his father's death, Richard Logan seems to have put himself and his estate under a greater financial obligation than he intended."

"Either could amount to thousands of pounds!"

"A powerful motivation to violence. Would you not agree?"

"Where did you discover this? How was it no one else knew?"

Foxe looked uncomfortable. "I haven't exactly discovered ..." he said, "... you see, they say love of money ... nothing else would really account for the stubbornness ... oh, I don't know ..." He shrugged.

The fine carriage clock on the mantelpiece chimed eleven.

"Is that the time? Forgive me, Alderman, but I must leave at once.

I sent a message to Mrs Baker saying I would arrive at eleven or thereabouts. She has the answers, I know. I must stop her lying to me. She's trying to protect some secret, of course, but it won't do any longer. No, it won't do at all. This time I'll have the truth, by God, even if I have to shake it out of her."

❧ 19 ❧

THE FIRST SECRETS

Foxe thought Mrs Baker's greeting showed considerable reserve. Perhaps she was simply tired of strangers in the house. The clerks conducting the inventory had been there, on and off, for several days. That was finished. The books in the library had been left for him to value and no attempt had been made to open the strongbox.

On his way from the alderman's house, Foxe had considered various approaches to raising the matters on which he was now sure he had been misled. Faced at last with a housekeeper nervous about what he might want to ask her, he made a rapid choice.

"Mrs Baker. Why have you lied to me? When did you discover your employer had misled you and stolen what was rightfully yours?"

The woman reacted as if he had struck her in the face. He pressed on without giving her time to respond.

"Your master — Mr Richard Logan that is — didn't take your keys or ask you to lock all the doors in the house save for the few in use. You decided to do that. It was only after he was dead that you concocted the tale of him taking and keeping the keys. I asked my own housekeeper to show me the keys she has. It was a substantial bunch, far too heavy for any man to keep on his person. For some reason, you

151

wished to delay Richard Logan from entering most of these rooms in his own house. The library and the small parlour were the ones you were concerned about, weren't they. Locking the rest was an attempt to draw attention away from those which mattered."

For a long moment, Mrs Baker neither moved nor spoke. Her face was completely drained of colour, but her eyes never left Foxe's. She was trying as hard as she could to guess what he knew and what she would be forced to reveal. At length she sighed and asked if she might be seated.

"It will be a long tale, sir, and I am not as young as I was."

"Make it a true tale, Mrs Baker. I am in no mood to be fobbed off with any more falsehoods or half-truths. I may not know quite all, but I assure you I know enough to see when you stray from the truth."

"I can see you do, sir. I am quite amazed at the amount you have discovered already. All I can hope is that you will forgive my clumsy attempt to mislead, once you understand the reason."

Foxe waited in silence. He was far from convinced by this sudden display of humility. Even now, he was sure the housekeeper was calculating the minimum that she could reveal and get away with.

"I must begin many years ago, when I was still a young maid in this household. Mr James was master then, and a fine master he was, not like his useless son. He was a true craftsman, Mr James. Everyone in Norfolk knew it. That was why the Earl of Brancaster hired him to undertake the remodelling of his house.

"From the start, Mr James told me, he and the earl formed a deep friendship. Both were quiet, thoughtful men. Both had developed an interest in antiquities, not just of Greece and Rome, but of the ancient peoples of Britain as well. Both had minds open to fresh ideas and eager for new knowledge.

"It wasn't long before the earl asked Mr James if he would be willing to work on a very special set of buildings to be erected in the grounds of the estate. From the outside, they must look like the temples, grottos and towers now so common as viewpoints and places to draw the eye. Within they would reveal a different purpose."

"What was that?"

"The earl had thought long and hard about the nature of this world, sir. He had also noted that certain figures and scenes were common in religious carvings and paintings throughout the ancient lands of Greece, Italy and Egypt. When he found similar idols and carvings in the remains left by the ancient Britons, he felt he had made a major discovery."

"Mr James told you all this, even though you were just a maid?"

"Not just a maid, sir. After his wife died, Mr James did not remarry. He had no need to. I was his wife in every sense but the legal one. Though we never had children, that was not for lack of the action that should have brought it about. I suppose that was a blessing in its way. He made me his housekeeper and had me marry the old butler, merely for form's sake and to throw dust in the eyes of the world. Mr Baker had no taste for women. The arrangement left him free to indulge himself in other directions."

"I see. And these buildings on the earl's estate were such as the world would not have approved?"

"Not in the current state of things. Towards the end of his life, the earl believed that the Christian religion was established and maintained by the forces of darkness and death. He said the Bible was obsessed with death and punishment. That the Christian horror at the so-called sins of the flesh was aimed at destroying the forces of light and life. As Mr James explained it, look where you would in the world of nature and you would find new life and growth which depended on the coming together of male and female. The sexual act was neither dirty nor wicked; it was the gateway to life itself. It was Christianity, and the Jews before that, who sought to bring all to death and servitude."

"Mr James believed this?"

"Most fervently, and so did I. Even after he began to lose his mind, he retained his belief in the earl's ideas. He had books in the library with engravings of discoveries dug from ancient sites. Statues of male gods with the horns of stags or rams and their virile members proudly erect. Carvings and paintings of people in the act of sexual congress, their faces filled with ecstasy. Representations of naked women seeking to arouse men to indulge in that holy act of generation."

"Like the statue in the library. Like the pictures he carved on the panels. Who was his model? Jane?"

"Not Jane, sir, me. Jane was far too young when she came to us. I was the one who acted as my master's model. I had a fine figure in my youth and was proud of his skill in capturing it in carved wood. The female figure in that statue is me, sir. I let you think Mr James carved it after his mind had gone, but it was done long before. Once it stood in pride of place on an altar dedicated to the God of Life in a temple in the earl's grounds."

"So how does it come to be here?"

"The earl died before his project was complete. With only Mr James able to work on the interiors of the buildings progress had been slow. The earl's son and heir had no time for his father's ideas. It was clear all would be destroyed once he came into his inheritance."

"So what happened?"

"There was a small group of men, scholars and philosophers mostly, who had gathered around the earl. They were not as some would have you believe, hypocrites who professed a convenient set of beliefs to allow them to indulge their lusts unchecked. They were honest, moral and learned men, most of them more faithful to their wives than a good many Christian believers. They knew all would be misunderstood. What was worse, they were sure the forces of death would seek to represent their discoveries as little better than pornography."

"I suspect they would have been right."

"They determined to conceal as many traces of their beliefs and practices as they could. Each took a portion of what they had held sacred or valuable — statues, pictures, various vessels and many books. Mr James brought that statue here, along with several fine silver cups and goblets bearing scenes of men and women coupling. He also brought a good number of books, which are still in the library upstairs, rebound so that the titles on the spines and the leather used will not give them away."

"You wanted to keep Mr Richard out of the library to prevent his greedy eyes seeing that statue as no more than an object that would fetch a good price in the hands of some wealthy rake. While Mr James was alive, it was safe. Afterwards ..."

"Mr James rarely left the library. As his mind failed, he became untrustworthy in the matter of candles and the like. That was when I determined to lock most of the doors. Mr James was generally content to stay in the library and do his carving and drawing, but I could not watch him all the time. Sometimes he wandered."

"How did you plan to protect what had been so dear to Mr James after he died?"

"I determined to stay here for the rest of my life. Mr Richard was afraid to drive me out, weakling that he was. I knew his terrible secret. How he had made a parody of his father's death. Oh, he made much of his sadness at the old master's decline, but I knew the truth. Richard Logan cared for no one but himself. He saw an opportunity to seize his father's wealth and took it."

All very plausible. True even. But still a smokescreen to deflect him from the major part of what she had been hiding. It was time to leave the past behind and come to those events which had provoked Mr Richard Logan's murder.

"What you have told me is very interesting, Mrs Baker, yet you have not answered my initial question. When did you discover Mr Richard Logan had been cheating you for so many years? Do not think me a fool, whom you can blind with more half-truths. I said I would have a full accounting and, believe me, I will, however hard you try to prevent it."

Without realising it, Foxe had risen to his feet, so that he towered over the woman sitting opposite him. This realisation almost caused him to draw back. He was not a cruel man. Threatening a defenceless, middle-aged woman appalled him. Yet to waver now would be to risk losing all. He forced himself to take half a step forward and raise his voice.

"Out with it, woman! You managed to see Mr James's Will, didn't you? You knew what it contained."

When the collapse came, it was total. Sobs, tears, howls of misery and despair. Was it real? This woman had already proved herself to be a clever actress. Foxe didn't know if he could trust her, even now. He'd rarely met anyone who was so quick-witted in a corner, or who could lie so fluently. Instead of rushing to help her, he sat and waited, hating himself for what he felt he had to do.

Finally, Mrs Baker composed herself sufficiently to continue.

"I never saw the Will, sir. I swear it! All I knew was what my late master and lover, Mr James, had told me. He said he had left me a substantial sum of money in his Will. Enough to leave service, rent a small house and live as a respectable woman for the rest of my life. I never received it. When I asked Mr Richard about it, he said his father was always promising things. It probably slipped his mind. That did not content me, so I pressed him — even threatened to consult a lawyer about bringing a suit against him. At length, he agreed, with great reluctance, that his father had made me what he termed 'a trifling bequest' in his Will. He hadn't been able to pay it yet, because his father's debts were too great. He had to discharge those first, he said. If I would but be patient, all would be well."

"Did you believe him?"

"Not one word. It was easier to get blood from a stone than extract money from Mr Richard Logan. Yet what could I do? I had no money for lawyers and courts. I did not even have any proof, merely the word of his father. In the end, I determined on another course. I would drive Richard Logan mad."

What kind of a woman was this? He knew her to be bold and confident. Was she capable of such sustained hatred as this? To become an avenging fury, remorseless in pushing a man over the edge into the hell of insanity? Yes, he thought she was.

"Every day since then I made his life a misery in a hundred little ways. I left him notes reminding him of his debt. I mended his socks with knots and thick darns that hurt his feet. I left his clothes and bedlinen unwashed for months on end. Tradesmen were always coming here with unpaid bills. He would tell me to keep them out. I would urge them to press him harder, then let them find him wherever he was hiding. He demanded that Jane should serve him his meals in my stead. I filled her head with tales of his lecherous ways with former servants until she would do no more than bang each dish down on the table and run back to the kitchen I even convinced her Mr Richard had made the carvings in the library as a way of assuaging the raging lusts that troubled him daily. In the end, he would run away to his beloved bells or shut himself in his parlour when he could not do that. All he had to do was pay me what I was due, sir. That would have brought an end to his discomforts."

"He could have had his revenge by selling that carving in the library."

"I hid it — and all else of my old master's work that I could find. It was not really the money I sought, but to see Mr James's wishes fulfilled and his wonderful creations preserved. His foolish son believed he could force me to yield in time. He could do little else, since he feared I would tell the world how he had used his father's illness to seize all for himself."

"And when James Logan died at last?"

"Nothing changed. The statue remained where I had hidden it. We ate less and lived in a cold house for the sake of economy, but that was a small price to pay for blocking Mr Richard's greed. Jane and I lived mostly in the kitchen, where the range kept us warm enough. The master's miserliness hurt himself mostly."

"He never tried to bend you to his will by force?"

"That milksop? He reckoned it was easier to wait for my death. Ha! I would have outlived him too. I have, haven't I?"

Was that a confession of murder?

"I kept the doors locked to prevent him from stumbling on the place where Mr James's treasures were hidden," she went on. "It has taken me some effort, while these clerks have been here, to keep moving them to prevent discovery. All but the carving, that is. I put it back in its place on the library table to celebrate Mr Richard's death. I will show the other things to you, sir, if you wish."

"Another time, I think, Mrs Baker, when I have the leisure to appreciate Mr James's artistry. Did Mr Richard indeed live only in the few rooms you claimed?"

"No, sir. He used only the one bedroom and dressing room, but all the downstairs rooms were open. I locked most of them when I heard of his death for fear of burglars. I left the dining room and bedroom open to divert the attention of people I knew must come to see the state of things."

"And that was why you lied about not having the keys?"

"Yes. I thought it would gain me time to check that nothing else had been left which might reveal the truth about Mr James. The library I could do little about. That's why I made up the story to explain the statue. I had a similar tale ready to cover the presence of the books showing the ancient gods, but you never asked me."

Foxe's mind was numb. How far from the truth his ideas had been. He'd more than half expected to find Mrs Baker was a callous murderess bent on taking revenge for being cheated by her employer. Instead, she had revealed a tale of such steadfast love it almost took his breath away.

"Were you really going to let Mr Richard's executors take that statue and sell it, Mrs Baker?"

"Of course not, sir. I can see you are too clever for me. Mr James carved two versions, but the wood cracked in the one the moment it was finished. It must have dried too quickly. That's the one on the library table. The second, perfect one is still hidden. In my Will, I have instructed that 'the wooden statue copied from the original in the library' is to be given to the mayor and corporation of the City of Norwich. I'm sure they'll hide it in a storeroom, but by then I will be beyond caring. What mattered all along was to put it beyond Mr Richard's grasp. That was all I wanted."

Foxe didn't know what to do for the best. All she had told him rang true. Whether, even now, it was the whole truth he had no means of understanding. In the end, he charged her to stay in the house and be sure not to destroy anything whatsoever.

What had become of Richard Logan's money?

❧ 20 ❧

THE POOR WEAVER

When Foxe returned home after his conversation with Mrs Baker, he said nothing to anyone. The rest of the day and all the next he didn't stir from the house, spending almost the whole time in his library. When evening came, Mrs Crombie hadn't seen him in the shop for three days and had begun to fret that she had upset him in some way. It wasn't that. His mind was too occupied for speech. The servants placed food before him, watched him eat it in silence, then rise and return to his library. They might as well have been invisible for all the notice he took of them. He stared at the wall, or through a window, sometimes muttering too quietly for anyone to make out the words. Each evening, he ate his dinner in silence, drank one or two glasses of brandy, still without a word, then shut himself alone in his library until he went to bed.

When daylight came again on that Wednesday morning in April, the weather remained warm, the sun was cheerful and the sky a mass of fluffy clouds against the blue. Foxe had eaten his breakfast with the window open, letting in the faint smell of growing things and the songs of thrushes and blackbirds. Once more, he'd uttered barely two words. While he ate, he stared out of the window. All at once he got up, called for his coat and left through the front door. He said neither where he was going nor when he would return. Behind him, the speculation began again.

Arthur Rogerstone, weaver and bell-ringer, lived in the Great Ward of the city known as 'Over the Water'. That was the area across the River Wensum from the cathedral and the castle, which had been settled by Huguenot people fleeing from a great persecution in the Low Countries in the time of Queen Elizabeth. The families included many skilled cloth-workers. The three small sub-wards of Coslany, Colegate and Fybridge were still the heart of the local cloth trade.

Foxe thought he knew his city well. The truth was that he rarely ventured far from his home and those of his friends and contacts. In the maze of streets, alleys, courts and lanes that formed the heart of Fybridge, he was lost. There were few people about in the streets either. During the hours of daylight, the inhabitants were working. The incessant clacking of weaving looms, placed on the top floors behind windows of abnormal length, was the only sign of the folk who lived there.

Eventually, helped by two old women seated on a doorstep and some children still too young to be employed beside their fathers, Foxe found the house he sought. There was the same long window just below the eaves. Here, however, the loom was silent. Mr Rogerstone was waiting for him.

In the period since Foxe had seen the man last — only a few days — Rogerstone had aged a decade. His face was grey with fatigue, his cheeks unshaven and his eyes ringed with the signs of a man who had slept little, if at all. Mrs Rogerstone offered refreshments, which Foxe accepted out of politeness, then swiftly withdrew. The parting look she gave her husband was eloquent of fear. Foxe assumed she doubted she would ever see him again.

Foxe was seated in the only good chair in the parlour. Mr Rogerstone was sitting on a stool opposite him. Neither had spoken since Foxe arrived. Foxe looked bored and Mr Rogerstone stared at the floor. When it began to appear they might both stay silent and immobile indefinitely, the weaver finally cleared his throat and began.

"I kn...knew you would come for me," Rogerstone said. The stutter was new. "I did my best to hide the tr. truth, but it was obvious I hadn't mi...mislead you, sir. I have waited for this mo...moment with dr...dread. Now it has come, there is a kind of relief. I will tell you all, sir. Then what will be will be."

"You went back to the ringing chamber a second time, after Mr Ovenden thought you had gone home."

"I did, sir. N...nor was I the only one. I saw someone sl...slipping out of the tower door as I arrived. Don't ask me who it was, for I do not kn...know."

"Several people went to the tower that night after the practice ended. None admitted it easily, just as you have not. Go on, Mr Rogerstone. Was Mr Logan alive when you reached the ringing chamber?"

"He was, sir. At first I could b...barely see him. One at least of the ca...candles set there had burned out and the others were almost sp...spent."

"It was a little while after your first visit then?"

"At least fifteen minutes. Ti...time enough for me to have reached T...Tombland and see F...Fye Bridge before me. That was when I turned back."

"Why?"

"I had f...forgotten my ...walking stick. The st...streets in this area are empty after dark. W...Weavers must rise with the dawn, sir, and work all day. Few have the t...taste for wandering the c...city in search of entertainment late into the evening. I was not that la..late in going home — the p...practice is usually ended before eight — but I always take a walking stick for d...defence. I am not a b...burly man, sir, as you can see."

"And that was the only reason for your return — to get your stick? What if the tower had been locked?"

"That would have been my ill luck. When I t...turned and retraced my st...steps I had no other intention, I swear. But as I went along another thought came to me. Ovenden and I are both w...weavers, sir. Our hands are our livelihood. If they were injured or maimed, what would happen to our families? Mine especially. Ovenden is a true craftsman, able to weave the finest stuffs. I am but a j...jobbing weaver."

"He is paid more than you are?"

"Much more. Yet he too f...feared any loss of earnings in these hard t...times. That was why we had decided to pl...plead with Mr Logan not to demand we take part in this peal he was pl...planning. We told you of 'The Bloody Peal', Mr Foxe?"

Foxe nodded.

"It was that Logan was set on repeating. He was a rich man and had no need to fear damage to his hands. As we t...told you before, sir, when Ovenden and I tried to explain why we could not take part in such an event, he flew into a great rage. Now, as I walked back to the tower, I decided I would r...refuse to take part at all."

"You expected him to be there to hear your decision?"

"To be honest with you, Mr Foxe, I did not. That was p ...partly why I could tell myself I was resolved on the matter. I did not expect to have to face him that night. Whether my c ...courage would have stayed firm until the next practice, I cannot say."

"But he was there."

"He was, sitting on a bench and breathing as heavily as if he had climbed to the roof of the tower moments before. He had his coat on ready to go home and his hat on his head, but he was not moving. He even had my walking stick held across his knees. When I entered, he looked up, but did not speak."

"What did you do?"

"Blurted out my decision. It was out before I realised what I was saying. All the way across the Market Place I had rehearsed my words, never dreaming they would be spoken. Now they had slipped out willy-nilly."

"What did Logan do?"

"He let out a great roar, then sprang up and dashed at me. The only words I could catch were that he would see me in h...hell before he would let me ruin what he had set his heart upon. He still had my stick in his hands. He swung it at me and struck me several cruel blows to my arms and back. My wife will confirm that I am badly bruised, sir. It has been essential for me to work these past days, but the pain has been almost too great to bear. Even breathing hurts."

"Did you fight back?"

"I am no fighter. My only thought was to defend myself if I could.

The man was beside himself with fury. I believe he would have killed me if he could. At first, all I could do was crouch and clutch my arms about me. Then my chance came."

"What happened?"

"Logan suddenly paused in his onslaught and stood stiff and still, his breath making a terrible noise — like a gasping and rattling. On the instant, I grasped my stick by one end and managed to twist it from his hands. I should have run away. Some devil inside me drove me to do what I did next."

"What was that?"

"I swung my stick with all the strength I had left and fetched Logan a mighty blow across his chest. He didn't bend over, sir, or even seem to feel the blow. He simply fell to the floor at my feet as a tree might fall in a forest, full-length with his arms clutching the place where I had hit him. Then I fled in earnest, convinced I had killed him. Did I commit murder, sir? I heard some say Logan's throat was cut, but I had no knife. It may only have been a rumour."

"It was true, Mr Rogerstone. Mr Logan's throat was cut."

"Then I didn't kill him?"

"I don't believe you did. However, we will return to that. Tell me first why you took his keys."

"Keys? What keys? I took no keys, sir, nor anything else, save my stick. The moment Mr Logan fell, I fled back down the stairs. I almost fell in my haste to be gone. I dashed out of the tower and away home with as much speed as I could make. But please, I beg of you, do not keep me in suspense. Did I kill the man or not?"

Rogerstone's agony was plain. Foxe barely hesitated.

"So far as I can tell, you did not. I cannot be completely certain yet, but I am sure you will never be charged with such an offence. You may be easy in your mind. If all you have told me it true, it is extremely unlikely that your blow caused Logan's death."

"Thank God! You cannot imagine the agony I have suffered. The thought that I had killed a man, even without intending to do so, has caused me greater wretchedness than the pain from Mr Logan's blows. When you asked to speak with me today, sir, I was certain you were coming to have me arrested and brought before the magistrate."

Foxe was glad to escape Rogerstone's house after that. The over-whelming expressions of gratitude from Rogerstone and his wife embarrassed him greatly. He had done nothing to deserve them, only allowed the man to speak the truth at last. He could be certain Roger-stone would never face any charges, because he doubted even an accu-sation of manslaughter could be sustained. Logan's throat had been cut after Rogerstone had left. How could that be ignored? No man recovers from having his throat cut open and being left to die in his own blood.

By the time Foxe had managed to find his way back to Magdalen Street, he felt too tired to return to his house on foot. As luck would have it, he was able to stop two chairmen who were taking their empty chair back into the heart of the city in hope of finding better chances of business. The empty streets around the weaver's houses were unlikely to offer them adequate pickings. They were happy to gain an unexpected customer. Foxe was delighted to be able to rest quietly and attempt to rearrange his thoughts.

How many more people had been to the tower of St. Peter Mancroft on that fateful evening? He had accounted for Ovenden and Rogerstone, then Napthorn and then Rogerstone a second time. There was still the mysterious woman. If it had been a woman, that is. The children thought it was, but it was dark. A man bundled up in a long coat or cloak might well resemble a woman from a little distance. Had someone else also gone to the tower, unseen by the children outside? What if Logan had suffered a bad injury from Rogerstone's blow and lain helpless on the floor until his murderer arrived? It would be a simple matter to cut the throat of a prone man.

So many people had told so many lies. Could he believe what he'd been told now? He had still not been able to eliminate Ovenden, Rogerstone and Napthorn as potential murderers on any basis save their own testimony. Mrs Baker too had lied to him, though now she claimed to have confessed the truth. Should he care whether he tracked down Logan's killer or not? From all he had heard, the man had been a miser who didn't hesitate to cheat the widows and families who paid him for coffins. Was the world any the worse for him leaving it?

Such were Foxe's thoughts as the chairmen bore him up the slope of Tombland, along Queen Street and London Street, until the noise and bustle of the great Market lay before them. It was not until they were passing the Guildhall, and his nostrils were assaulted by the smell of the Fish Market, that Foxe recalled the matter of the keys.

Was the woman the children saw a whore plying her business and nothing to do with Logan's death? Was it a man they mistook for a woman? If he — or she — had been the last person in the tower with Logan, had he — or she — taken his keys and used them to enter the house afterwards?

By now the chairmen had reached Foxe's house and set him down outside his front door. He paid them the agreed fee, added two pence each for their extra labour in bearing him uphill for such a long way, and sent them off full of expressions of gratitude. He should have gone inside to rest, but his mind was in too great a turmoil. Instead, he turned past the fine bow windows of his shop, adorned once again with a range of the latest printed caricatures from London, and pushed open the door. Perhaps talking to Mrs Crombie could help him work things out.

Happily for Mr Foxe, if not for the profits of his business, there were no customers when he entered. Mrs Crombie was seated in a chair brought in from the stockroom, giving Charlie a reading lesson. Foxe was reluctant to interrupt this worthwhile activity, but both declared the lesson at an end. Foxe knew they wanted more than anything to catch up on his latest news. It was better to satisfy their curiosity than leave them to waste their time in fruitless speculations. He would give them a summary, at least.

"Well?" he said when his tale was done. "Can either of you suggest what happened to the keys Mr Logan must have had with him? Or who the mysterious woman might be who spent so long in the tower that evening? If it was a woman, of course."

"The street urchins would never mistake one for the other, Master," Charlie said.

"Not in good light, I agree," Foxe said. "But it was dark and they were some distance away."

"Not even then. Any pickpocket needs to know what he's dealing with. Women don't keep their money in the same place as men. Any whore had better be sure who she's approaching too. Even beggars will take a different approach to a man than a woman."

"I agree with Charlie," Mrs Crombie added. "Besides you only need to see the person's legs and feet — and their heads. A man may wear a long cloak — though I've seen few in this city who do. He's much more likely to wear a coat that barely reaches below his knees. No woman will reveal so much of her legs in public, not even a lady of the night. No man will go out in a skirt either."

"What do you mean about seeing the head?" Foxe said.

"On a cold evening, a man will wear a hat. A woman is more likely to wear a bonnet, or a cloak with the hood drawn over her head. You would need to have very poor sight to confuse them."

"What about a man trying to pass for a woman?"

"Maybe, but why? What would such a man gain? Unless you're used to wearing a skirt, it would be cumbersome to move in, especially if you knew you must climb a spiral staircase. I suppose it's possible, but there would have to be a very strong reason. Do you know of one?"

"No," Foxe said. There was nothing else to add.

Neither Mrs Crombie nor Charlie had any other ideas. They were as puzzled as Foxe that so much information had led to so little progress. After a moment, Mrs Crombie changed the subject.

"We have missed your visits, Mr Foxe. Your servants assured us you were not ill, but could give no other explanation."

"I have been ... preoccupied, Mrs Crombie. That is all."

"If that's all it is ..."

21

BREAKTHROUGH

Foxe found himself sinking further into gloom as the evening progressed. He did scant justice to the excellent dinner his cook had prepared for him. Then he drank too much brandy for a man dining alone, so that his steps were unsteady as he made his way to his bed.

It may have been weariness, or more likely the brandy, that caused him to fall at once into a restless sleep. All evening, he had gone over and over what he had discovered about the death of Richard Logan. He felt in his bones he was on the brink of finding the solution, yet it continued to elude him.

His mind must have continued to grapple with the mystery while he slept. Sometime in the middle of the night, he woke suddenly, his mouth dry and sour but his brain wonderfully alert. It was as well he was alone, for he sat up in an instant with a loud cry.

"The keys! The strongbox keys!"

What a blind fool he had been. No man would carry such keys around with him, no matter how much of a miser he might be. Slumping back on the pillows, he let his mind supply the details.

The locksmith had told them Logan's strongbox was of an unusually secure design. Not only was it made of iron, probably an inch or more thick, it needed two keys to open it. The locks these keys fitted were also well down below the metal of the lid; too far from the keyholes for picklocks to reach them. The locks would also be especially strong ones, of that he was sure. Wouldn't the keys have an intricate shape to fit the many levers of such locks?

Those keys too were missing. That much had been known for days. They had all made the foolish assumption Logan had them with him. Yet not only would they be large and heavy, they would also have unusually long shanks and be far too large and heavy for a pocket. Where would Logan keep them? Hidden somewhere in the house, of course.

Where?

Mrs Baker had told them Logan spent a good deal of time in the small parlour. It was in the closet off that room where he'd had the strongbox placed. Didn't misers like to be close to their money? What else was in there? A desk. Its drawers had been locked, since the locksmith had to open them. Logan must have kept his desk keys with him. They would be small and easily carried. Was that why his keys had been stolen; so that someone could open those desk drawers?

No, that wouldn't work. The person who entered the house using those keys was frightened away almost at once. He had no time to open the desk, let alone find the strongbox keys.

Where would Logan have put them? Not just in a locked drawer surely. Too easy, with the strongbox only a few feet away. Yes! In a secret drawer. Most desks had at least one.

Blocked again. The locksmith knew all about secret drawers. Foxe had wandered upstairs to the library, but Halloran and Bonnard had stayed in the parlour. They told him later the locksmith had located two secret drawers in the desk. Both were empty.

Then it hit him. The housekeeper had fooled him yet again. Alderman Halloran had declared no one could be more cunning than his friend Mr Ashmole Foxe. He was wrong. Twice Mrs Baker had proved too quick for Foxe in inventing plausible stories to cover her actions.

She would not do it a third time.

BY THE TIME MR FOXE LEFT HIS BED THE NEXT MORNING, HE KNEW
exactly what had taken place in the tower of St. Peter Mancroft; how
Richard Logan had died; and the parts each person who had been
there had played in bringing about that death. What still eluded him
was why Logan had been assaulted and his throat cut. Who had done
it he thought he knew, but not why. There was still at least one crucial
element to be discovered. He was determined to find it out that day.
He had had enough of lies and evasions.

After breakfast, Foxe went at once to Logan's house. Jane opened
the door to his knocking and stood back to let him enter. It was as if
she had expected him. She pointed to the door to the small parlour,
then returned to the servant's quarters.

Mrs Baker was waiting. She even had cups ready for coffee. She said
nothing, though her eyes never left his face. Jane returned with the
coffee, Mrs Baker poured Foxe and herself a cup, then waited until
Jane had gone.

"I have waited here for the last two mornings, sir, for I knew you
were bound to come sooner or later. I see from your face that you have
found me out. I did my best, yet you have proved too clever for me.
When last you came, I sensed you were almost possessed of the truth.
It has been a fine contest, in its way. Now, though I never thought to
say this, I am glad I have lost. I need no longer carry the crushing
burden that has lain on my shoulders these past few days. Where do
you want me to begin?"

"With Miss Hester Logan," Foxe said. "You must have known her
well."

"I did. I am only a few years older than her — six or seven, I think.
She never knew her mother, so I was the only woman she could turn to
as she grew up. Unlike her brother, she never resented my closeness to
her father. Never claimed to feel shame that he had those relations
with me that were due to a wife."

"What happened to make her father turn against her?"

"What has befallen many a motherless girl. As she moved towards
womanhood, she became moody, even rebellious. She loved her father

dearly, as he loved her, but somehow she could not resist pushing against the restrictions he imposed on her. She fancied herself fully grown and able to make her own choices."

"Including the choice of a husband?"

"Especially that. I tried to guide her, but she turned away. Then a rascal of a man, the youngest son of Colonel Pannier of Alvingham Hall, set his sights on her. He needed money, for his family had precious little. Knowing Mr James was wealthy, he set out to seduce poor Hester. It was easily done. He was well used to women and she was ignorant of the duplicity of men. They eloped and he sought to force her father to provide a fat dowry as a condition of marriage."

"Mr Logan refused."

"Flatly. Beneath the irritation and rebellion, father and daughter were devoted to one another. It can be terrible when love is corrupted into anger. Mr James felt betrayed and his daughter complicit in the affair. I tried to make him see sense, but the hurt ran too deep. When the seducer, seeing no money was forthcoming, abandoned her, her father refused to take her back."

"But you stayed in touch with her?"

"As best I could. Her father's attitude made her feel betrayed too. She swore she would never set foot under this roof again. Still, she had no quarrel with me. When we could, we wrote to one another. I could not receive her letters here, of course. A friend in the town agreed to receive them on my behalf."

"So you followed her progress."

"It was hard at first. She had been a pampered gentlewoman. Now she had to turn a servant to survive. She even spent time in the work-house. Her letters became sporadic, then ceased. I guessed she had no more leisure to write, nor money to pay for any letters I sent her. Only when she married Napthorn did things become easier. Then her letters recommenced. He was a good man and treated her well. Yet even from the start his health was uncertain. It was plain he would never make old bones."

"Her father's attitude never softened towards her?"

"Oh yes it did, sir. I worked on him constantly, though I could not admit that Hester and I had stayed in touch. In time, he regretted his harshness and wanted to see his daughter again. But he made a dreadful mistake."

"What was that? All he had to do was tell you of his change of heart and you could have told him how to get in touch with her."

"He didn't realise I knew where she was. I just told you, sir. I didn't think I could tell him of our correspondence without the risk he would believe I had betrayed him too."

"So what did he do?"

"He asked her brother to find her and bear a message. Neither of us realised the full measure of Richard Logan's character then. Mr Richard went to King's Lynn, spent some days there and returned with the news that he had found his sister. She was married, he said, and wanted nothing more to do with any of us."

"Was this true?"

"I don't know what he said to her, but all my work to bring about a reconciliation was undone. I sent letters, but had no reply. Then Mr James descended into madness and the opportunity to bring them together was lost. For years, he forgot he had a daughter, confusing her with the wife who had died so long ago."

"Did Miss Hester never resume contact?"

"She did, sir, about two months past. That was when I learned she had a son, the only survivor of all those to whom she had given birth. She also told me her husband had died and she had left King's Lynn to move north. Her son, Silas, was a sailor who worked mostly from South Shields. She had given up her house in Norfolk and moved to be with him, since he had not yet married."

"Did she explain why she broke her silence?"

"She was lonely. Her son was away at sea for weeks at a time. She knew almost no one amongst the neighbours. She was melancholy enough to write that she was weary of life itself. Her husband may have loved her dearly, but he proved a poor provider. In her widowhood, she must exist on a pittance."

"How did you reply?"

"With both joy and sadness. Joy because she had turned to me in her distress. Sadness because I had to tell her of her father's death. Yet even that was not all bad news. I knew he had tried to bridge the gap between them. If his mind had not collapsed, he would have made provision for her in his Will. I explained that much of his money was gone, but I was sure her brother would find some way to assist her in her need. Since then I have heard no more."

"Her son was the man who came here on the day of the murder to speak to Mr Richard and was turned away. But you knew that."

"I recognised the name he gave me when I let him in. There is also a good deal of his mother in his face."

"He told me that he came to Norwich to speak to his uncle and ask for help."

"I guessed as much. I also guessed how he would be received. That was why, as he was leaving, I told him the master would be at St. Peter Mancroft that evening. If he waited until the others had left, he might catch him alone where he could not be turned away. As Tower Captain, the master was always the last to leave, often staying a while to tidy up, snuff the candles, and leave all ready for Sunday."

"Did he say he would go?"

"He just nodded, but I saw him outside the house a while later, so I guessed he would follow the master to be sure of the way."

"You determined to go as well."

"I said you were cleverer than I am, Mr Foxe. Now I see how far you have penetrated the fog of lies I hoped would lead you astray. Yes, I decided to go too."

"Before I left my house to come here, I heard from one who has examined Mr James Logan's Will. His son lied to you all. His father left substantial legacies both to you and to his daughter. They were never paid, I know, but they still stand."

"He had been using those lies on all of us for years and we had all been deceived." She turned to look straight into Foxe's eyes. "Now I know better."

"How do you know, Mrs Baker? I guess you have seen inside that strongbox. How did you open it? I'm sure Mr Richard hid the keys well."

22

DEATH OF A MISER

For a few moments, Mrs Baker was silent. Foxe did not hurry her. He could only guess at the anguish she had suffered. Now he couldn't find it in his heart to condemn her actions, or even the many lies she had told him. All she had done had been driven by love — even those final moments in the ringing chamber as the candles guttered out. If he could, he would have spared her. Walked away and pretended he was beaten. What kept him in his chair was the fear that an unsympathetic judge and jury would convict a stranger not just of theft, but of a crime he had not committed. Mrs Hester Napthorn deserved better than to learn her only son had been convicted of murder.

Mrs Baker raised her head at last, took a deep breath and wiped the tears from her face with the handkerchief she was clutching.

"He did, sir. Very well. I will tell you how his guilt was finally made plain to me. If ever a man deserved a mean and violent death, it was Richard Logan. The Good Book says love of money is the root of all evil. He must have been an evil man indeed, Mr Foxe, for few have loved money as much as him.

"I killed Richard Logan," she said. "Now I shall go to the gallows myself. I do not regret what I did. All I regret is that poor Jane must face the future on her own. How she will cope without me, I cannot tell."

"We will come back to that," Foxe said. He showed no surprise at what she had said. He had expected it when he came. Instead, in a voice as calm and steady as a man asking for a fresh cup of coffee, he posed a fresh question. "What made you wish to kill him?"

Mrs Baker gave a great sigh. "Must I go on, sir? I am so very tired."

"You must. We are almost at the end. Then you can rest."

"About three weeks ago, the master told me one morning that he was going to his workshop for an hour. I thought nothing of it at first. He had been doing something in this very room, as he often did on days when he stayed indoors. Usually, if he was called away, he would close the door before he left. That day he left it open, and as I walked past I saw something else. He had left his bunch of keys on the desk."

"Which keys did he carry?"

"Only the keys to the front door and the keys to his desk. He was fanatical about keeping his desk keys to himself. They were never out of his possession."

"Did you guess why?"

"Of course. I knew he must have the keys to his strongbox hidden somewhere in the house. They are too large to be carried. The most likely place would be in his desk, since he kept it locked whenever he was not sitting at it."

"You decided to look."

"I know it was wrong of me, sir, but I had wondered about that strongbox for a long time. Why did he need such a large and secure place of storage? What did he keep in there? His father never had such a thing in the house, not even when his fortunes were at their peak."

"What if he returned unexpectedly?"

"My only chance was to act on the instant. If he noticed his keys were missing, he would hurry back at once. It took only a moment to open the locked drawers of the desk and see no keys were there. You will know such desks often have secret drawers. I knew this one did. Mr James had shown them to me once, long ago. The whereabouts of the first I recalled easily. There was one of the strongbox keys. The other key must be in the second secret drawer. In my haste and excitement, I could not remember where it was."

She was reliving those frantic moments now. Her tiredness had fallen away. She was leaning forward from her chair, staring at the desk which had been the site of the events she was describing.

"I wasted precious seconds searching to no avail," she went on. "Then I remembered. I opened the second drawer and had both keys. I jumped from the desk chair and went over to the strongbox. The keys fitted easily. They must have been used often. However, the iron lid was much heavier than I had expected. It took me most of my strength to lift it."

"What was inside?"

"Guineas, sir. Guineas and sovereigns. Nothing but gold coins, right to the brim. The master claimed his father had lost or spent all he had earned, leaving us almost penniless. Lies! Nothing but lies! There must have been thousands of pounds in that box. No wonder the floor of the room sloped towards it and the master had warned us never to venture into that part of the cellar that lay beneath."

"Did you take any?"

"Of course not. He probably counted them regularly. He would have known at once if I had taken even one. I shut the lid, locked it, and put the strongbox keys back where I had found them. Then I put his own keys back where he had left them. I was barely in time. I had reached the hallway when the front door flew open and the master rushed in. I could hear his sigh of relief and his rattling of the locked drawers from where I stood."

"You knew now for certain how Mr Richard had lied to you."

"Indeed. For a while, my brain was in confusion. I hated him even more than before, yet there was nothing I could do. He wouldn't make the same mistake with his keys again. I couldn't confront him without making plain what I had done. In the end, I decided to wait and hope some opportunity would arise to cause his ruin."

"Did you think Silas Napthorn's coming was that opportunity?"

"I did not know. Much depended on the outcome of any meeting between them. That was why I did all I could to bring it about."

"You were determined to overhear that conversation."

"Of course. After the master left that evening, I knew I had to follow him. Between the time the young man came to the house and the master left, I went shopping. At an apothecary's, I bought a small bottle of laudanum. I mixed some of it into the drink I gave to Jane. She complained of the strange taste, and I scolded her for allowing her imagination to run away with her. Of course, she soon began to feel tired and dizzy, so I told her to go to bed. You probably have a cold, I said. You'll feel better in the morning."

"Why drug her?"

"I didn't want her involved in whatever might happen. I could brazen matters out, secure in the knowledge that the master feared I would one day reveal how he had laid hands on his father's wealth. He could dismiss Jane without a character at any time."

"You didn't fear going out in the dark?"

"It wasn't so dark. The bell-ringers met from six in the evening until seven or thereabouts. Even when they left, it would still not be fully dark. Besides, if you recall, the moon was only just past the full. It had been a fine day too, so the sky was clear. There would be light enough to see by, yet sufficient shadows to conceal me should I need them."

"What happened? Leave nothing out, Mrs Baker, I beg you. Some of it I know already, but you are the only one who can complete my knowledge."

"I reached the church just after the practice had ended. As I came up alongside the churchyard, I could hear voices, then saw the men dispersing. There were many words of farewell and a good deal of laughter. I was about to go towards the church door, when I saw two of them turn back and go inside again. They must have forgotten something, for they came out again after only a few minutes. One went off towards The White Swan Inn. The other passed all too close to where I was crouched behind a large tomb.

"I waited a moment longer, then took my chance to cross the churchyard and slip inside the tower. I decided to wait there, close by the door, so that the master would not leave me locked inside. I would be able to hear him coming down the stairway and creep out again before he came into the space under the tower. Since he would need to lock the outer door, I could make sure of reaching this house before him.

"I could hear his footsteps above me, so I knew he was still there. That was when I saw Mr Napthorn come in. Either he had misjudged the time, or he had seen the other two men and made sure they were gone before he came."

"You could see all this well enough?"

"Certainly. St. Peter Mancroft has many large windows, sir, and the moon was already shining through one of them. It was dim inside, but still light enough to see something as large and pale as a man's face.

"Mr Napthorn didn't know where to go, though he must have heard the footsteps overhead as well as I did. I crouched down in a corner, in a terror lest he should stumble on me, but all was well. He found the door to the spiral stairs and began to climb."

"What did you do?"

"I went after him, as quietly as I could. The door to the ringing chamber was open and I could see the light from the candles inside. Quick as I could, I darted past the opening and sat on the turn of the stairs above. I could not see, but I could hear all.

"Mr Napthorn must have told the master who he was before I reached my hiding place, for I heard Mr Richard begin his litany of excuses, his claims of abject poverty, his hypocritical declarations that only lack of means had prevented him from acting before. To my delight, Mr Napthorn brushed all this aside. He said his mother was in such dire need that even a small amount would suffice. He knew Mr Logan to be the owner of a good business who lived in a large house. He must have the means to offer at least something, if only out of Christian charity.

"To my surprise, the master at once broke out into one of the rages for which he was becoming notorious. He cursed and swore in the most hideous manner, never minding that he stood in God's House. He called his sister filthy names, shouted that she had made her choice by her rebellion all those years ago, and declared she should have nothing of his, even if she lay dying in the dirt before him.

"I could hardly believe what I was hearing. I almost leapt up to confront this monster of cruelty, but Mr Napthorn burst out of the doorway and rushed down the stairs. If he had turned his head, he would have seen me, but he did not."

"Did you go in to your master, as you said you wished to do?"

"Not then, sir. I could hear him cursing and swearing inside the ringing chamber. To be honest, I was afraid. He was a big man, sir. Alone, I would be helpless should he decide to strike me down. Then I heard more steps below. I thought young Mr Napthorn was returning.

"It was not him. I did not know the man who came. He went into the chamber and I heard my master demand to know what he wanted. Whatever it was I could not hear, for his voice was low and uncertain. Yet it was enough to bring back Mr Richard's rage in full measure. He called the man a wretch and a snivelling coward — aye, and much worse. I would blush to repeat such words in front of you or anyone. Then I heard a great stamping and a sound like a maid makes when she beats a carpet. Twice or three times that came, then a pause, then another great blow and a clattering like someone falling. The man I had seen rushed out and nearly fell down the stairs in his haste to get away.

"Again I waited, but all was silent. That worried me more than the noise. I imagined the master creeping through the door to seize me before I could leave. Still, my determination proved stronger than my fears. I stepped into the room meaning to heap my own curses on this foul deceiver. Let him hurt me as he might, I would have told him to his face how much I hated him."

She paused again. Each word seemed wrung from her at the cost of the last dregs of her energy. Foxe waited, hardly daring to breathe in case she could not go on. Then she shook her head and rallied what reserves she had left.

"It was almost dark inside. The candles had nearly burned out. Just two still guttered and smoked. It was by their light that I saw the master lying full length on the floor with his head away from where I had come in. He was wearing his coat, as if he had been about to leave when he fell. His hat and wig had tumbled off and lay beside him. Then I saw a knife whose blade gleamed in the remains of the candlelight.

"It was the sight of that knife which was my undoing, sir. Even now,

I scarcely know what came over me. Overwhelming loathing for this creature lying before me, I know. Yet also love. Love for my poor Hester, so cruelly deceived by her brother. Love for my James, whose life and wealth had been forfeited to his son's greed. Even love for Jane, whom I had tricked so that I could be where I was.

"I swear I was in a kind of daze as I snatched up the knife. I raised the master's head and slashed open his throat. Then I felt in his pocket for his keys and ran for dear life."

Mr Foxe said nothing for a moment, then once again asked a question.

"Did you find much blood on you afterwards?"

"No. That surprised me. There was only some blood on the hand that had held the knife. Blood I surely saw, thick and dark, but all spilled onto the floor. What I did must have killed him, Mr Foxe. No human being could survive such a tear as that knife had left in his throat.

"There, I have told you all and confessed to the worst of crimes. You may lead me away to face my punishment, for it is richly deserved. Do not allow Mr Napthorn to be accused of what he did not do. He does not deserve the title of murderer. I do."

"No, Mrs Baker," Foxe said. "You do not. You did not kill Mr Richard Logan. He was already dead."

Foxe barely moved fast enough to catch her as she fell from the chair in a dead faint.

🦊 23 🦊

EXPLANATIONS

T he next day passed with Foxe still wondering how much of the truth he should disclose. There were some aspects of Logan's miserable existence which should be forgotten. The man was dead. No need to allow his greed and dishonesty to reach out from the grave to blight the lives of the living.

To Mr Tate therefore, he offered only the assurance that he was sure none of the bell-ringers were involved. Since the peal Logan had set his heart on would not now take place, there was no need to share the concerns of Ovenden and Rogerstone with anyone else. As it was, George Tate was so relieved by his assurances that he no longer cared who might have killed Logan. All that mattered was that none of his friends had done it.

In the city, Logan's death had already faded from anyone's interest. Most people, if they thought about it at all, assumed a thief or vagrant had found the tower door open, gone inside to see what he could steal and been surprised by Logan. Foxe saw no need to correct this tale.

Brock, Mrs Crombie and the others were a different matter. They had given him invaluable help and deserved to know the truth — or at least as much of it as he could share.

First, Foxe called Charlie into his library and gave him a version of

180

the facts suitable to his age, if not his intelligence. He had no doubt the boy would soon fill most of the gaps in the story by a combination of his own wits and artless remarks to Mrs Crombie. Then he sent him out with a purse full of pennies to distribute suitable extra rewards to the street children.

The three people now seated in the library, engrossed in his tale, had contributed most to seeing it solved. Mrs Crombie was there, of course, leaving Miss Benfield in charge of the shop. Brock had come too, while Alderman Halloran had excused himself from a meeting with the mayor and the Guild of Tallow Chandlers to be present. Now, as Foxe's explanation drew to a close, they began to press him with questions.

"So who actually killed Logan?" Brock asked. "I must have got lost and missed that somewhere."

"They all did — and none of them too," Foxe said. "We can leave Mrs Baker out. Gradnor, Ovenden, Rogerstone and Napthorn each contributed to his death in different ways. They caused Logan to suffer a series of towering rages. Those, coupled with his scuffles with Napthorn and Rogerstone, taxed his body until it gave way. He died of natural causes, probably an apoplexy or a bursting of the heart. If the coroner had asked for a more thorough examination, this would have been clear. As it was, he saw a man whose throat had been cut and assumed that was the cause of death."

"What convinced you that it was not?" Alderman Halloran asked.

"The blood — or rather, the lack of it. Had the great veins and arteries in his throat been severed while his heart was still beating, the blood would have spurted out in a fountain. It would have splashed all around, maybe even up the walls. But all agreed there was only a pool of blood on Logan's breast and under the body. That meant his heart had stopped beating before any blood began to flow. His body was lying face down, so blood flowed out due to that, not the pumping of his heart."

"Who cut his throat then? It must have been Rogerstone, since he was last to leave." Brock's mind was still occupied by reaching a final solution.

This was the most dangerous ground for Foxe to try to skip over.

He was determined to conceal Mrs Baker's part in the affair if he could. If the alderman knew the truth, he might feel compelled to seek advice on whether a charge should be brought against her. He was a magistrate after all. Foxe had included the story of her going to the church and overhearing the final conversations. He had concealed her confession by suggesting she ran away as soon as Rogerstone left. Now he had to find a way to avoid Brock continuing to dig until the truth was revealed.

"Even if he did, it was no murder, as I have just explained. We cannot even be sure he was the last person to leave. Once Mrs Baker had left, we have no witnesses left. Anyone could have gone in through the open door. Remember, we have never found Logan's personal keys. All those men I mentioned as having been there deny taking them."

Foxe held his breath. He knew perfectly well who had taken Logan's keys. He had used them himself yesterday to slip the keys to the strongbox into new hiding places. Later he would get someone to help him "discover" those keys where he had put them. The house was full of small recesses, boxes, vases and other ornaments well suited to concealment.

"Yes," Mrs Crombie said. "I was wondering about the keys to the strongbox. They're still missing, I believe. Do you have no idea where they might be?"

He could not tell the truth. Mrs Baker had opened the strongbox and removed a hundred guineas after Richard Logan's death. She thought at least that was her due. Now she would receive far more under the terms of James Logan's Will. He hadn't asked her to put them back. She'd promised him she would give them to Jane to help her while she found a new position.

"Jane and I are to lose our home," she'd told him. "Neither of us has any money set aside. I reckoned the master owed us at least that amount. No one save him knew what the box contained, so I reckoned no one would miss them. I can give them back to you."

"Just give me the keys," Foxe had told her. "If you are found with those, suspicion must fall on you. You told us when we first came that only the master had the bulk of the house keys. Give them all to me and I will claim to have discovered the 'missing' desk keys also somewhere about. As for the gold, I never heard you mention it. Just be as surprised as I shall be when the strongbox is opened and the contents revealed."

Now Foxe could see Brock pondering what Mrs Crombie had said, deciding how to probe further.

"This is all I can tell you," Foxe said, before Brock could speak. "Rogerstone swore he hadn't taken Logan's keys. We know they had come somehow into the hands of the person who used them to enter Mr Logan's house later that same night. Both Jane and Mrs Baker were clear someone had come in through the front door, roused them by the noise, then run away when he saw them coming into the hallway from the servant's quarters. It wasn't Napthorn. He entered later through the window in the scullery. I didn't ask Ovenden. Still, there was no evidence Ovenden had returned to the tower after he left The White Swan. Of course, there was no evidence he hadn't either. So many people were creeping about that night! I still haven't been able to make any sense of it. All I can assume is that Mr Logan dropped them on his way to the ringing practice, probably near his house. Someone saw him do it, picked up the keys and tried his luck later. Where they are now, heaven knows. Of course, the strongbox keys won't be with them. Too big and heavy. I'm sure we'll find those somewhere in the house, if we look hard enough."

It was an outrageous tissue of lies, but the best he could think up on the spot. Would they accept it? Mrs Crombie was looking dubious.

The alderman saved the day for him. "I agree with you, Foxe," he said. "There's no proof of anyone's guilt that would be sufficient to convince a jury. Many believe already that the murderer will never be brought to trial. Let's leave it at that. It will also bring the benefit that James Logan's memory need not be sullied by the discovery of his son's evil nature."

Spoken like a true politician Foxe thought. When a semblance of the truth will serve to avoid aspersions on a famous figure, it is preferable to leave it that way. Norwich was proud of James Logan. His son would be soon forgotten, along with the questions of who killed him.

At last Mrs Crombie managed to ask a question. "What of Mrs

Baker's health, Mr Foxe? You said she fainted while talking to you. Do you know what caused it?"

Foxe was delighted to change onto another subject.

"Fatigue and stress. I called for Jane, of course, and together we carried her to her room, where she could be laid on the bed. She had begun to revive almost before we got her there. I was greatly relieved by that, I can tell you. Not just for the sake of the lady's health, but because I feared Jane was about to fly at me and tear my face with her nails. She only grew calm again when Mrs Baker assured her that the event was not of my making. I have been back to the house twice since then — in the morning and the evening yesterday — to seek news of Mrs Baker's progress. She kept to her bed in the morning, Jane told me. Or rather, that was what she wrote on her slate. When I went in the afternoon, I was able to talk with Mrs Baker herself."

"What does she intend to do? You have told us Mr Logan left all his estate to pay for new bells. I presume it must therefore be sold. Mrs Baker and Jane must leave."

"As you say, he has not left anything for Mrs Baker or Jane. However, remember the legacies under his father's Will were never paid. He said there was no money to do so. I am sure that was a lie and we'll find a good deal of money hidden away, if we look hard enough. Mr Bonnard believes the money Logan refused to give to Mrs Baker and his sister must be paid by right of the father's Will. I am inclined to agree with him. What do you think, Alderman?"

"I'm no lawyer, but I cannot see why his father's wishes should not be honoured. It was the son who frustrated his intention by claiming there was not the money to pay for it. From what you tell us, Foxe, that is probably untrue. As an executor, I would be inclined to treat those bequests as unpaid debts to be settled before fresh bequests can be made."

"I think it must be somewhere," Foxe said. "Richard Logan was such a miser he would never have spent it. If the strongbox contains money, for example, the amount would be substantial. It is not a huge box, but I would say it's near three feet high and two feet across."

"I'm amazed the floor can support it," Brock said. "It must weigh almost a ton."

Foxe laughed. "You're right, Brock. The floor does bend downwards a little as you reach it. No joists alone could withstand such a weight. Jane fetched me a candle and I went into the cellar. Whoever installed the strongbox built a pillar of bricks below to support it. It's a rough piece of work, but it's done its job."

"Why would his wealth be in coin?" Halloran could not envisage anyone hiding his wealth in his house. "His father was wealthy, but I recall that he owned some lands under crops and several properties in the city."

"I think the son sold them secretly, once he had seized control of his father's estate. His nature was to be obsessive. Maybe he feared poor harvests might lessen the land's value. Houses require expenditure to keep them in good condition. Logan wanted to be famous amongst the only people he valued, the county's bell-ringers. I have no idea what, say, six or eight new bells might cost, but it would be a substantial sum. My guess is he converted his father's investments into gold, pleaded poverty to excuse his subsequent miserly actions, and kept all hidden where it could not lose value. It was the first of his mistakes."

"Why do you say that?"

"He destroyed the bulk of his own income. His father could no longer earn anything. He was supposed to be dead. Under Richard Logan's direction, I doubt that business of his ever made much of a profit, even though he cheated his customers. He tried to limit all expenditure, I know, but I expect he still had to use some of the wealth he tried to hoard."

The questions began to slow after that. Most were mere points of clarification. Although Foxe had presented most of the elements of the tale, it was good to take in all the twists and turns.

Alderman Halloran, naturally, wanted Foxe to look out for suitable books for him when the library in Logan's house was sold. Brock worried about the fate of Silas Napthorn. He would be convicted of theft and face severe punishment, if the judge and jury did not appeal to the king for mercy.

"He's an experienced seaman," Brock said several times. "Put him in the navy. Too good a man to waste." He only stopped returning to the point when the alderman said he had already asked the mayor to send a message along those lines to whichever judge would be passing sentence. At last they fell silent and Foxe breathed a sigh of relief. It was high time to forget about bells and carvings and everything else associated with the Logan family. It was a long time since he had felt so wearied at the end of an investigation.

24

OF CATS, MICE AND JOURNEYS

I f Foxe felt he had reached the end of his involvement with Logan's murder, he was mistaken. Next day, he discovered his audience had been mulling through the details overnight and finding fresh areas that needed to be probed.

Mrs Crombie was the first. Foxe wandered into the shop on his way home from his morning visit to the coffeehouse to find her waiting for him. The customer she had been serving left as Foxe entered, so there was nothing to prevent her starting her questions right away.

What did Mrs Baker and Jane intend to do about finding somewhere to live she wanted to know? How would they manage for money? Before Foxe could pronounce a word in reply, she added more questions. How would Mrs Hester Napthorn cope, if her son was sentenced to death, transportation or naval service? Could she manage without him? Would it be possible to send her some money from what was owed to her to tide her over?

Fearing yet more demands for details, Foxe held up his hand to stem the flow. "I don't know anything specific about Mrs Napthorn," he said. "No one here does, save her son. It's even possible he has been exaggerating her problems to improve his chances of a lenient sentence. Mrs Baker's plans, and how they affect Jane Thaxter, are matters she has shared with me. Whether I should tell anyone else ...."

Seeing Mrs Crombie take a deep breath and open her mouth for another onslaught, Foxe gave her no further space to speak.

"What I can tell you is that she wishes to go to South Shields as soon as possible to discover the truth for herself. I cannot think it would be a problem for the executors of Richard Logan's Will to let her take a draft for an interim payment, as you suggested. I also know Mrs Baker believes that, with her help, Mrs Napthorn can live the rest of her life in health and vigour."

Mrs Crombie managed to slip in another question before Foxe could prevent it. "When will she leave? Do you know that?"

"The barrier to her departure, as I understand it, is Jane. She has never been out of this city. Naturally, she's fearful of the long journey north and the prospect of being amongst unfamiliar people and places. As you know, she cannot speak. Some people are cruel and thoughtless in dealing with unfortunates like Jane. Here, she is known to all the people she must deal with. Strangers terrify her. Mrs Baker, of course, will never go and leave her behind alone. She is therefore trapped."

"Not at all, Mr Foxe. I have a solution to her problem. Without Eleanor, I am finding it hard to work here all day, then attend to my household chores when I get home. I am also lonely. I admit it. Thanks to your generosity, I can afford to employ a maid to ease the burden upon me. If she is willing, Jane Thaxter may come to work for me on a live-in basis. Once she is settled, I can easily make use of her here in the shop as well on occasion. As I'm sure you know, books attract dust in the way cheese attracts mice. If she spent a little time cleaning and tidying here, she could gain confidence in dealing with people she does not know. I am sure our customers would react to her with kindness. If they did not, they would find the door locked against them."

Foxe agreed this might indeed be a suitable solution. He would put it to Mrs Baker and arrange for Mrs Crombie to meet Jane. He did not much care for the idea of locking the door on any customer, but he hoped this was not a threat he should take literally. If Mrs Crombie's displeasure was not enough to bring about a change of attitude, he was sure his own would be more than sufficient.

Foxe was about to turn away when Mrs Crombie laid her hand on his arm to detain him. He recognised that determined look she always assumed when she wanted him to agree to something she had already set her heart upon. His heart sank.

"Speaking of mice," she began. "You may not have noticed, but they have become all too common on these premises. Some have desecrated literary classics with their urine and droppings. Others have taken to raiding our stores of certain lozenges, medicinal herbs and powders sold by the ounce. Only this morning, I found they had chewed their way into a bag of violet cachous and nibbled several of them."

'Indeed? Well, at least we will have mice with the sweetest breath in Norwich."

"You may mock me, Mr Foxe, but I am serious. Mrs Whitbread, your cook, tells me they have become a plague to her as well. I gather a smoked ham she was storing now has upon it the marks of mouse teeth."

Foxe waited. He guessed what was coming.

"I wish to obtain a cat, Mr Foxe. It can live in the shed behind the storeroom and have free run of all the rooms at night to catch its food. One of my neighbours has a cat which has just had some sturdy kittens. I am told the mother is an excellent mouser, so they may well inherit the skill."

"A cat?" Foxe did his best to sound doubtful. "Might traps not be a simpler expedient?"

"Will you set them each day and remove the results afterwards?"

"Surely Charlie can do that?"

"What is your objection to a cat, sir?"

The addition of 'sir' made Foxe realise he was in danger of provoking her too far.

"None whatsoever, Mrs Crombie. I am rather fond of cats."

"Then I will obtain suitable kittens."

"Kittens? A cat, you said. That to me implies only one."

"One for here and one for Mrs Whitbread's kitchen and larder. You might also like to install one in the rest of your house. I'm sure there are mice there as well."

"How many kittens has your neighbour's cat given birth to, Mrs Crombie?"

"Six, Mr Foxe, and such darling little beasts —"

"Two will be quite sufficient. Mice flee from even the smell of cats, so I'm sure two will be enough to rid the whole place of the plague."

Having at last managed to escape any further requests or questions, Foxe was understandably dismayed to discover Captain Brock enjoying coffee in his library courtesy of Mrs Dobbins and Molly. Like most sailors, Brock had long experience of the best ways to charm ladies when he wished to do so. Foxe's female servants nearly worshipped the man and squabbled amongst themselves over who should serve him refreshment. Even young Florence was catching the disease. She had been seen on at least two occasions to slip past Molly to serve Brock's coffee herself.

Brock it appeared, was also primed with an additional question. He had noticed what he took to be a gap in the story Foxe had told them the day before.

"Who was the man who went into Logan's house late that evening, Foxe? The one who let himself in with what we all assumed were the keys he had stolen from Logan's body? Do you really not know?"

Foxe hesitated, then decided to take Brock into his confidence. "He doesn't exist. There was no such man."

"But Mrs Baker told you —"

"Mrs Baker is quick to invent plausible lies when the need arises, Brock. I will tell you this in the strictest confidence, you understand. The last thing I want is for any suspicion to fall on Mrs Baker. I did tell you all that she had also gone to the church that evening. What I left out will answer your question."

"You have my word I will say nothing, you know that."

"Mrs Baker did not want Jane to get involved in any way. She was safe from Richard Logan's malice. Jane was not. She'd urged Napthorn to go to the church and determined to be there herself when he did. It was best if Jane knew nothing about it. Mrs Baker naturally expected

Logan to come home in a great rage and try to discover how Napthorn knew where he was."

"That makes sense."

"That afternoon, she bought laudanum and gave some to Jane, hidden in a drink with her dinner. She planned to leave her asleep and slip out secretly. She was longer at the church than she expected and she came back a good deal upset by what she had witnessed. I imagine she made too much noise coming in. Jane is a light sleeper, so she awakened and came to see who it was, still partly under the influence of the drug. In an instant, Mrs Baker pretended the noise had been due to an intruder going out, not her coming in. She said she too had come to see who it was, only to find Jane had frightened him away. Jane believed her. That was what Jane wrote for us on her slate when the alderman and I asked what she had seen."

"An answer for everything, Foxe. I should have known."

Foxe smiled.

WITH THE INVESTIGATION COMPLETED, EVERYTHING IN THE FOXE household should have gone back to the way it had been before. The master should have resumed his daily routine, visited the theatre regularly, and just as regularly entertained young women in his bedroom. In fact, none of this came about. Somehow, with that sixth sense servants have for the vagaries of their employers, they realised a shift had taken place. Its exact nature was as yet unclear, but they were certain it would change their routine on a permanent basis.

Mrs Crombie and the others in the bookshop also felt a change in the air. When Mr Foxe appeared, his manner was muted, as if he was never more than half present. Miss Benfield thought he was saddened by the approaching departure of his friend, Captain Brock. The captain had told them he would be away a long time — a year at least, in his estimation. Charlie thought his master was getting old. He must be more than thirty by now, so it was inevitable that he would lose his gaiety and turn ponderous in his manner. Mrs Crombie found herself unreasonably worried by small things. Foxe's sudden conversion to a more conservative style of dressing. His tendency to stare about him as if uncertain of what to do next. The way he would pick up a book, turn one or two pages, then set it down unread. He reminded her, she told her cousin, of a swallow in autumn. Aware of the coming winter, but not quite ready yet to hide away wherever swallows went.

Truth to tell, Foxe himself could not have told anyone what was wrong; only that he was seized by a restlessness uncertainty about the future. A sense that the way he had lived until now would no longer be suitable. What he wanted, he did not know, only that it was not to stay as he had been.

He even tried a visit to the bagnio once run by Gracie Catt. When she moved away, the woman who took over as madam was not at all to Foxe's taste. There was always something fawning and insincere in her manners. He also suspected that she bullied her girls. Gracie had treated them as a family rather than a profit-hungry owner relying on servile employees. Business declined a good deal and many of the long-established clients went elsewhere. Foxe himself had sworn never to return while that woman was in charge.

Now circumstances had changed and he decided to give the new madam a fair trial. She was very different from the sophisticated and urbane Gracie. A plumper woman and far less aristocratic in appearance. A motherly shoulder to cry on rather than an elder sister to look up to. Still, she greeted him without affectation and summoned her girls for him to make his choice. They were cheerful, well-dressed and appeared happy, winking and smiling at him to influence his choice. Several arched their backs to make their bosoms seem fuller. One blew him a kiss.

In the end, his choice fell on one of the less flamboyant of the group. A girl of maybe nineteen or twenty, neatly dressed, pretty in a homely way and with a trim figure rather than a lush one. To Foxe's considerable delight, she proved well experienced in the ways of pleasing men, as well as surprisingly athletic. Since he was as skilled in arousing his partner's passions as her, they spent a lively few hours together, before Foxe admitted exhaustion and his companion, her hair and face wet with perspiration, rested her head on his chest and fell asleep, one arm stretched across his stomach. It was all very satisfactory, yet still not quite enough to raise Foxe's spirits to the level he craved.

Foxe also started attending the theatre again, much to the manager's relief. As soon as he saw him enter, the man rushed up, full of apologies for what happened the last time Foxe had been there. Young Miss Smith, it seemed, had come near to losing her place in the company, thanks to her outburst. She had only been retained because she had become a favourite amongst many of the younger blades who came almost every night.

The man's fawning apologies annoyed Foxe. "There was no need for anyone to censure Miss Smith," he said, showing his anger. "She had done nothing wrong. I do not even know if she was laughing at me. It so happened that I was in a poor mood that evening and took her action too much to heart. If anyone was at fault, it was me. If it had crossed my mind that you would threaten her with dismissal from the company, I would have come before now to register my disapproval. Is she performing this evening?"

The manager, much dismayed by Foxe's rebuke, admitted she was not.

"I will send her a note, apologising for what happened," Foxe said. "Remember that this is a theatre, not a house of assignation. I admit I have enjoyed the favours of some of your actresses before now, but I have always been careful to ensure none have been under any obligation to accept what I suggested. Keep it that way, sir. Times are changing. Men will always pursue pretty, young actresses. Some will enjoy their attentions, but others will no longer see submitting to wealthy men as essential to advance their careers. In tragic roles especially, talent should count for more than anything else."

When he thought about it later, Foxe realised how much his attitude had changed. He had been one of the worst offenders in considering young actresses as material for his amusement, much like a person choosing a kitten to make into a pet. Hadn't his own household referred to the parade of young women passing through in just that way? It wasn't that he regretted what he had done, yet that style of life no longer possessed the same attraction. He would probably never be virtuous in any conventional sense, but he could at least find a greater sense of purpose to accompany his peccadilloes.

One day near the end of the month, when Foxe was sitting in his library, trying to read a volume of the memoirs of a famous explorer, there was a timid knocking at the door. It was Charlie.

"Sorry to bother you, Master, but Missus Crombie says that Colonel Rathbone is in the shop complaining the book he ordered is still not come. He's a right old misery and hates having to deal with a woman. She wonders whether you could come and talk to him."

Foxe stretched and looked for a slip of paper to mark his place in the book. Colonel Rathbone's complaints could go on for hours. He would still be in full flow when Foxe arrived. Best to let him exhaust some of his bile first.

"Very well, Charlie. Go back and tell Mrs Crombie I will come in a few minutes."

"Can I ask you something first, Master?" Charlie said. "Is Miss Lily ever coming back? She was always kind to me. She's got a lovely bum too."

Foxe attempted to look severe. "Don't let Mrs Crombie hear you talk like that, my boy, or you'll never hear the last of it. Besides, you're too young to be having such ideas. Your time will come, I have no doubt of it. Just not yet."

"But is Miss Lily coming back?"

"I doubt it, Charlie. People who work on the stage lead wandering lives. She went to Bath, I believe, but now I've heard she's in Dublin. Even if she returned, she will have changed. She may even be married by now."

"Do you think so? Women are strange creatures, aren't they? They claim to like you, then they want to change you."

"How have you reached that conclusion? I don't say that it's wrong, but I'm surprised to hear you saying it."

"It's Missus Crombie. I heard her tell you once that she liked me for my cheeky ways and willingness to do as I wished. Now she's always lecturing me on proper behaviour and telling me off when I talk as I used to."

"That's different, lad. She's teaching you the correct ways to behave. If your mother had been equal to the task, I'm sure she would have done the same."

"Do you think so?"

"I do. The important question is whether it will have any effect?"

"Only in her presence, Master. Not always then."

"I thought as much. Mrs Crombie means well, Charlie. Please don't upset her more than you have to. When you do, she blames me for being too lenient with you."

"She doesn't cuff your ears though."

"Not yet anyway. She can hurt them enough with complaining."

"Everyone wonders why you haven't married her, Master. There's a good few men who come into the shop who haven't come only to look at the books. Someone else might get there first."

"I'm not sure I'm the marrying kind, lad."

"That's what I told Florence."

"Florence? The kitchen maid? She's what — fourteen — and you're only just twelve. That's rather young for marriage, isn't it?"

"She's got her eye on me, Master. Don't you doubt it. She smuggles me treats from the kitchen and all. She even offered to kiss me good-night. I don't discourage her mind, but I'm wise to her just the same."

Foxe could no longer contain himself. Happily, Charlie thought he was laughing at Florence and joined in. There you are, ladies, Foxe thought. Try as you may, Charlie and I may both escape you yet.

After that, Colonel Rathbone was despatched on his way with a briskness that left him bewildered rather than angry. Mrs Crombie was grateful for the respite to her ears, since the Colonel had never lost the habit of speaking as if he were addressing his regiment before battle.

⬥

"I HAVE DECIDED TO GO TO BATH," FOXE TOLD BROCK ONE DAY about a week later. "It will not be a long trip. I'll be back before you leave for Italy. I need to recover my strength and good spirits. Maybe this sluggishness indicates an imbalance in humours; a slight excess of black bile, perhaps. A short course of taking the waters should clear it up."

"What about your business?"

"Mrs Crombie will manage perfectly well without me. I've asked Mr Bonnard, the attorney, to keep an eye on my other interests. He's a clever man and has welcomed the business. If you can be away for a year, I should have no problem being absent for three weeks or a month."

"They'll all miss you. Mrs Crombie especially. Charlie too."

"I'm sure they'll cope splendidly. Look how they managed when I was so wrapped up in the business of the bell-ringers."

"Have you heard anything from Mrs Baker?"

"She wrote to tell me she had reached South Shields safely and found Mrs Napthorn somewhat recovered, though greatly worried about her son. I've promised to let them know what happens at his trial. Since it's his first offence, I'm almost sure he'll be sentenced to death, as the law decrees, then have his sentence changed to service in the Royal Navy for seven years or so."

"I hope so. When do you plan to leave for Bath?"

"In a few days or so, no more. The change will do me good, if nothing else. I'm getting stale and bored."

"What you need is employment," Brock said. "I know you don't need the money, but you do need something to occupy and challenge your mind. Why not let it be known, amongst people of the right sort, that you'll assist with any serious problems or criminal actions they might face? You do it for Halloran and the mayor. You've just done it for those bell-ringers. Why not make it something of a profession?"

"Would anyone be interested?"

"Of course they would. Wealthy people always want to know of anyone who will relieve them of unpleasant demands. In confidential matters, they'd never turn to anyone right outside their class, but you're a kind of gentleman by grace and favour. You're more than rich enough to qualify, you have proper manners, and you move easily amongst the gentry. You've proved yourself to be discrete too. They'll feel at ease speaking to you, because they know they won't be risking the family secrets being shared with all and sundry. You make them feel comfortable, while still allowing them to think themselves superior because you're 'in trade'. That's a combination sure to win favour."

"I don't know ..."

"Think about it while you're in Bath. You might also think about asking Mrs Crombie —"

"Have you considered approaching Lady Henfield — ?"

Both held up a warning hand, glared at the other, then burst out laughing.

'The Bloody Peal' was a genuine occurrence which took place on the date mentioned in the text. At the time, it was considered an amazing feat, both of endurance and memory. It would be considered extremely demanding even today.

Norwich in the eighteenth century was one of the foremost centres of the art of change ringing outside London. The church of St. Peter Mancroft, on the edge of the Market Place, still has an excellent peal of bells, just as it did then.

AFTERWORD

Did you enjoy this book? If you did, and have a brief moment or two to spare, I would be so grateful if you could leave a brief review, either on your local Amazon website or Goodreads. Your help in spreading the word about Mr Foxe and his friends will be invaluable and deeply appreciated. Reviews make an immense difference by helping new readers find the series and enjoy them as you have. Even the shortest review can be influential. People are often put off by the word 'review', but it can be as short and to the point as, "I loved it. You will too." Thank you.

This is Book 3 in the series "The Ashmole Foxe Georgian Mysteries".

What links these books together is their protagonist, Ashmole Foxe, and their their setting in Norwich, England, in the 1760s. Although there are some series elements, each book stands on its own and can be read without reference to the previous volumes.

PREVIOUS BOOKS IN THIS SERIES

Book 1: "The Fabric of Murder"

Norwich in the 1760s is one of the largest and most prosperous cities in the realm. Its wealth comes from a booming trade in the famous "Norwich Stuffs"—fine worsted cloth, often richly dyed and embroidered. So when a leading cloth-manufacturer in the city is murdered and his business seems on the brink of collapse, there is a real fear that a forced sale of his huge stocks of cloth will ruin the trade for everyone else. Who killed him? Who is the strange, unknown, but apparently wealthy man who is trying to secure the dead man's stocks to sell overseas? What role do the London cloth-merchants play in the tragedy?

With no kind of organised police force beyond a handful of rough, uneducated constables and night-watchmen, the mayor and aldermen are forced to turn to Mr. Ashmole Foxe. They ask him to unravel the crime, bring the killer to justice and save the city's most important and profitable trade from imminent collapse; all in record time and without upsetting the delicate balance between the manufacturers in Norwich and the merchants in London who provide the bulk of their orders.

Book 2: "Dark Threads of Vengeance"

In this second book in the series, Mr Ashmole Foxe, Georgian dandy, bookseller and confidential investigator, finds himself alone and way out of his depth. The mayor is demanding he find the murderer of a prominent merchant and banker before the city is crippled by financial panic; Alderman Halloran is hounding him over the theft of some of his favourite books; and his much-loved companions, the Catt sisters, have left Norwich, unlikely to return. Poor Foxe has no clues, few ideas and very little hope.

The dead man, Joseph Morrow, was both a prominent and unbending puritan and a constant preacher against the evils of alcohol. So why did his body reek of cheap brandy? What caused his corpse to be found in the hold of a wherry, moored in a little-used and down-at-heel area by Fye Bridge? And what could such a pompous, self-righteous and rigidly Christian man have done that would provoke someone to murder him?

MORE BOOKS ARE PLANNED

You can keep track of progress at my website, "Pen and Pension", where you'll also find regular blog posts about Britain and Norfolk in Georgian and Regency times.

ABOUT THE AUTHOR

William Savage is an author of historical mysteries. History has always been his fascination, but it had to wait for him to retire to have the time to turn this love into a popular blog and two growing series of historical novels.

You can find out more via his Amazon author page here.

ALSO BY WILLIAM SAVAGE

I also write a series about another character in Georgian Norfolk: Dr Adam Bascom. These are set during the wars against Revolutionary France and Napoleon, and in the county outside Norwich.

Book 1: "An Unlamented Death", set in 1791.

"An Unlamented Death" starts the series. When, Dr. Adam Bascom trips over a body in Gressington churchyard, he never imagines it will change the whole direction of his life. Adam's curiosity and sense of justice cannot accept the official cover-up, so he uses friends, old and new, unexpected contacts and even his own mother to help him get to the truth.

Book 2: "The Code for Killing", set in 1792/3.

In "The Code for Killing", Dr Adam Bascom is called to Norwich to treat a young man who has been assaulted and left with total memory loss. Other mysteries follow. Someone murders a King's Messenger. Secret government papers go missing. A local miller appears to have been killed twice! Adam must disentangle intrigue and lies to find the code.

Book 3: "A Shortcut to Murder", set in 1793.

Dr Adam Bascom just wants to get back to his medical work. Fate, however, seems determined to keep him off-balance. His brother, Giles, is called upon as magistrate to investigate the death of Sir Jackman Wennard, rake, racehorse breeder and baronet. Adam is soon convinced it was murder, so agrees to help his brother find the killer.

Printed in Great Britain
by Amazon

12713508R00123